DUKE UNDONE

The Castleburys
Book 2

By Jennifer Seasons

© Copyright 2024 by Jennifer Seasons
Text by Jennifer Seasons
Cover by Dar Albert

Dragonblade Publishing, Inc. is an imprint of Kathryn Le Veque Novels, Inc.
P.O. Box 23
Moreno Valley, CA 92556
cco@dragonbladepublishing.com

Produced in the United States of America

First Edition March 2024
Print Edition

Reproduction of any kind except where it pertains to short quotes in relation to advertising or promotion is strictly prohibited.

All Rights Reserved.

The characters and events portrayed in this book are fictitious. Any similarity to real persons, living or dead, is purely coincidental and not intended by the author.

ARE YOU SIGNED UP FOR DRAGONBLADE'S BLOG?

You'll get the latest news and information on exclusive giveaways, exclusive excerpts, coming releases, sales, free books, cover reveals and more.

Check out our complete list of authors, too!

No spam, no junk. That's a promise!

Sign Up Here

www.dragonbladepublishing.com

Dearest Reader;

Thank you for your support of a small press. At Dragonblade Publishing, we strive to bring you the highest quality Historical Romance from some of the best authors in the business. Without your support, there is no 'us', so we sincerely hope you adore these stories and find some new favorite authors along the way.

Happy Reading!

CEO, Dragonblade Publishing

"Deuce it, Winston, why must you insist on being the voice of reason and reality?" Joss muttered with a grimace, and sliced his valet a disapproving glance. "Verily, one crisis at a time is enough to contend with. It is not the time to remind me of my father's financial incompetence and the duchy's dusty coffers. Nor is it the time to mention the state of my theatre venture."

"Is there a correct time to mention such things?"

Point, Winston.

"'Never' is a good time that comes to mind."

"Of course, Your Grace." Oh, that note of disapproval. He heard it. Loud and clear.

"I endeavor to reside in a state of denial, as you well know. Gentler on my conscience that way. Follow me." Joss waved for his valet to follow him and strode with sure, purposeful strides along the ornate hall carpet worn thin with age and down the grand staircase to the main floor of Barlow House in search of coffee and something to eat. A rather unfortunate consequence of possessing such a large and fit physique was the constant hunger that hounded him like a sporting canine on the scent of a fox. From dawn until dusk and back again his stomach demanded nourishment, often diverting him from one task or another in search of sustenance.

"Walk with me. I've an inclination to see if Bower has that new round of scones ready." Joss had already consumed the previous batch. His cook, a white-haired, ruddy fellow from the north counties, well understood that Joss required breaking his fast with a full, hearty meal first thing in the morning—and then he required another full round an hour later. Such was his appetite.

Winston, short of stature and wide of girth, huffed in short, shallow breaths, and hustled to catch up with him. With thick fingers, the valet nudged his round wire spectacles up his nose and settled them back into place. "Might I mention once again, Your Grace, that you are uniquely sized in stature and that your stride is also of unique size?

Chapter One

June 1832
Barlow House
Mayfair

SOME INDIGNITIES A man could suffer.
This was not one of them.
"What in *bloody* hell am I looking at?"

"Well, Your Grace, it would appear... ahem... to be a reproduction of your likeness... in charcoal, perhaps... in which you seem to be..." Winston, the most loyal of valets, turned his head this way and that, brow furrowed in befuddlement as he studied the bit of parchment Joss held in his hands. "Why, you appear to be quite nude and... ill-equipped, shall we say, to... *perform* in this artist's visual rendition of Shakespeare's *Romeo and Juliet*."

Perfect. Exactly what Joss needed at this moment in time. He raked a hand through his thick mane of tawny hair and looked about his bedchamber, barely noting the sumptuous furnishings. "This ruffian, this *Anonymous* artist, has come after the wrong duke," Joss growled, and crumpled the sketch in his fist. "Bullying me, taunting me with this juvenile sketch. I'll not bite."

"But, Your Grace, if this scoundrel artist looses upon London a compromising portrait of yourself, as they claim a desire to do, shan't that have dire consequences for your success in acquiring silent investors for your theatre? Investors you sorely need?"

And that I am not, in truth, as vigorous a person such as, are my legs even a fraction as long?"

The corners of Joss's finely drawn lips twitched, but he kept walking, shrugging a broad shoulder inside his velvet jacket w. affected nonchalance, knowing it would rankle his most proper valet. "Perhaps I should slow to a snail's pace? Would that better suit?"

An indignant sniff. "Not all of us are so abnormally large as to require a draft mount upon which to ride. Some of us are rather average. Portly, mayhap. But average, all in all."

Chuckling lightly, Joss admired, as he often did, the paintings hung along the open, elegant stairwell walls and the way the soft morning light filtered through the massive, sparkling windows and kissed them with delicate warmth. And as he also often did, Joss mused that it was a shame no one had rendered the scene onto canvas with oil and paintbrush for him to appreciate when those dreary, gray English mornings rolled in, as they were wont to do so often come late autumn and throughout the winter and spring months. He should commission someone.

"Your Grace?"

Joss descended the last stair, stepping with a polished Wellington to the marble floor of the spacious townhouse entryway. "Gomery," he said to his butler, noting the tray Gomery held aloft in his white-gloved hands, and altered his direction to intercept the elderly servant in powerful, long-legged strides. "Is that what I think it is?"

"It is the latest edition of the *Gazette*, Your Grace. The most recent Revivalists attack occupies the front page."

"Of course it does." Muttering as a chill dashed down his spine, Joss reached for the newspaper, scanning the front page for the report. "Says here they terrorized the docklands and the Thames River folk drinking at the Prospect of Whitby." Having endured a close encounter with the murdering group of masked noblemen in recent times himself, Joss was in absolutely no rush to repeat the experience.

"Rather a shame, if you ask me, that the Bow Street Runners were unable to apprehend any of them after that lunatic absconded with Lord Castlebury's eldest daughter," Winston commented, and sniffed again—a habit he indulged in when displeased. Which, in truth, was decidedly often. "At least the kidnapper, that vile Lord Arnold, is deceased."

"Few know of Lady Amslee's horrific ordeal, as she has requested it to remain that way." Joss raised a bronze, aristocratic brow pointedly at his valet. Winston's penchant for idle gossip was well known amongst all in residence at Barlow House. If ever in doubt about the latest *ton* squabble or whose lady's maid was recently discovered in her employer's bedchamber after dark, Winston could clarify with certainty in mere moments. His uncanny knowledge was awe-inspiring and rather terrifying at the same time.

"I've the utmost respect for the viscountess, Your Grace, you know that." Winston tsked and cut him a brief, disapproving look. "She has been nothing but gracious when in attendance here at Barlow House."

Joss furrowed his brow, glancing up from the unsettling Revivalists article, narrowing his unusual golden eyes slightly in speculation. "And how often has the viscountess been a guest here at Barlow House, pray tell?"

"The Castleburys have been guests upon numerous occasions over the years, Your Grace, before you assumed the title," chimed in Gomery, his voice raspy with age as he shuffled across the pale marble floors toward Joss on creaky, protesting knees. "The whole lot of them. Lord and Lady Castlebury and their sons and daughters, including the new viscountess."

Castlebury daughters.

Joss instantly scowled, and his stomach tightened with dislike and something else—something frustrated and agitated and prowling—as the image of one highly vexing Lady Ceranora Castlebury flashed across his mind. *"Minx,"* he growled.

"Beg pardon?" Winston inquired archly, brushing an invisible speck of something off the front of his tailored brown waistcoat and sniffing again, no doubt taking issue with Joss's word choice regarding a lady of the peerage.

"Don't get your trousers in a bunch, man. I was referring to that insufferable chit, Lady Ceranora Castlebury. Trust me when I say that one does not deserve your defense," Joss insisted, recalling the sharp rap of her boot heel against his shin when he'd merely been acting the properly concerned gentleman, returning her safely home and saving her from her own poor judgment when he'd discovered her in a pub in Covent Garden late one night. Unescorted. In disguise.

Troublesome chit.

Gorgeous.

"It is of little consequence," he muttered, snapping the crisp pages of the freshly printed *Gazette* and glancing once again at its contents. "Where was I?"

Brushing past his servants, Joss followed the pull of the morning light filtering so alluringly through the dining room windows, washing the oak floors in an enchanting amber glow. He noticed things like that. Light, affect, *mood*. Naturally, as consequence, the theatre drew him like flowers drew bees, ripe with the promise of sweet nectar. For him, that nectar was the utter deliciousness of the written and performed word. For as long as he could remember, his head had filled with visions of the way tales should be acted each time he picked up a book and read what was within. Even bloody boring tomes at Eton. His mind simply saw the scene, *knew* the setting and how it should unfold onstage.

"Your Grace, I'm certain you're quite aware, but this is the dining room. You break your fast in the drawing room," Winston reminded him, gesturing to the floor above them, his tone direct and the slightest bit affronted at the clear break from expected behavior befitting one of Joss's elevated station.

Joss's lips twitched at the corners, and he coughed, covering the laugh rising in his chest. "Of course." What would he do without his valet to keep him on the side of propriety and good manners? "Thank you for saving me from my heathen ways."

"It's a difficult task, that." The consternation in Winston's tone nearly ruined his composure. Rankling his valet never ceased to amuse and entertain. It was so *easy*. Like fruit ripe for the picking.

"I agree! Hedonistic, loose-moraled barbarian. Shame on me." Joss held out his hand, palm down, and affected a contrite expression, though he wasn't in the least. "Here now, slap my hand."

"I would never!" gasped Winston, his brown eyes widening with shock and offense as his hands flew upward, landing one on top of the other against his hearty chest. "The audacity of such a thing!" His face turning an interesting shade of reddish purple, he spluttered. "Why, you are a *duke*!"

"Last time I checked, that's correct." Oh, his valet's reaction was entertainment personified.

"Stop jesting before you give the poor fellow heart palpitations," Gomery chided, his rheumy eyes bright with amusement. "You know how seriously he takes everything."

"Which is precisely why it is so much fun to rankle him." Giving up pretense, Joss laughed, the sound deep and easy. "You're a good sport, my man."

"Well." Sniffing and snapping his lapels with furious little flips of his wrists, Winston spun on his heels. "If that will be quite all, I will check with Bowers on the state of scones."

"That's more Gomery's department, my good man." Joss inclined his head in his butler's direction. "Let him see to it."

A barely concealed huff this time. "If you will, Your Grace, I would prefer to see to them myself."

"Oh, stop being such a wet blanket and sit with me." Joss waved at an ornately carved dining table chair, its mahogany glossy with recent cleaning. "I've something I wish to discuss."

"I'll see to that second breakfast, Your Grace."

"Thank you," Joss called out as he glanced over his shoulder at a slowly retreating Gomery. "Bugger," he muttered, realizing how long it could be with Gomery at the helm before he received said second breakfast. His stomach growled, immediately protesting. Perhaps he should have let Winston huff his way to the kitchen to see about his food after all. "That was not well-planned."

Instead of sitting at the long, elegant dining table with his valet, Joss strolled leisurely to the large front windows draped in rich blue curtains and looked out onto Upper Brook Street, for the time being ignoring his grumbling stomach. Clasping his hands behind his back, he watched as Londoners strolled by on their way to and from Hyde Park. Having been in the Rainville family for several generations since its construction in seventeen forty-three, Barlow House possessed the distinguished location of one of the closest townhomes to the park. That, in turn, provided Joss quite the vantage point from which to observe the goings-on of the *ton*. Human nature had a way of revealing itself in small, subtle moments. Such as the twitch of a brow, the pinch of a mouth, the swivel of a head when a certain other passed by. All those little tells. For Joss, it was theatre and drama—all outside his windows.

"You wished to speak with me, Your Grace?"

Turning his attention from a young miss trying valiantly to catch the eye of a dapper-looking buck as he chatted with a small group of chums under the lush canopy of the tree across the street, Joss nodded. "I did. We need a plan to catch Anonymous before they release any sort of painting about me—nude or otherwise. I've meetings with potential investors next week, and I want this inconvenience dealt with immediately so I may give that my full attention and effort."

"Understandable." Winston nodded from his position at the ridiculously long dining table Joss's mother had purchased from a renowned German maker when he had been a lad of twelve. His father had fumed over the extravagant cost, but one promise from his mother to fill every seat at the very next dinner party had smoothed the duke's ruffled feathers.

His parents had loved to entertain. His father, quite lavishly. Foolishly. Until there was nothing left when Joss inherited the title. Quite the surprise it had been to discover the condition of the duchy's coffers after his father's passing. Though, to his father's credit, he had settled his debts before his death last year and relieved Joss of the headache of settling them himself. His gambling and lavishness had simply left nothing else for Joss or the tenants living within the estate's bounds that relied upon their landlord for the care and upkeep of their homes. Who relied upon the estate's vast agricultural fields for gainful work. And who relied upon work at mills owned by the Duke of Somerton.

Through wit and ingenuity, Joss had created a way to fix the imbalance. To right the wrongs. With his theatre and its proceeds, he would, with hard work, right the course and open the flow of abundance once again. His tenants would once again know security and comfort, have dry roofs over their heads.

"I've the best actors in London, without doubt. The theatre itself is magnificent and decadent. And I've nearly convinced Thatcher Goodrich to exclusively write his plays for my theatre. It's quite the feat, you know, and I've almost accomplished it. King William himself proclaimed Goodrich the greatest playwright of our time. Did you know the king's mistress was quite the actor herself, once upon a time?" Joss touched two fingers to his lips and raised them and his eyes briefly skyward, murmuring, "Rest well, Mrs. Jordan, you brilliant creative goddess."

"Indeed, I had heard that," Winston replied lightly. "Now, about this rascal painter." Pursing his lips thoughtfully, he crossed his legs and laced his fingers together over his knee. "It seems to me that to catch the scoundrel, you must lay a trap."

"Agreed." Tapping a finger against his chin, Joss turned once again to the bay window overlooking Upper Brook Street and the tiny garden of Barlow House contained quite tidily behind a black iron fence. Nothing more, really, than a narrow bed of flowers retained by a wall of marble that dropped straight down to the basement windows below. The four-or-so-feet gap between the windows and the marble wall allowed light into the rooms below ground—and the ability to open the windows to receive fresh air through the stifling kitchen area. "We must ensnare them. I propose we put your most impressive communication skills to use."

His interest keenly piqued, Winston's eyes brightened instantly. "Why, I think that's a rather excellent idea! I do so love putting those particular skills to use. They are my favorite, after all," he said with a mischievous grin, his earlier pout completely forgotten.

"Oh, I know." Did Joss ever. Because of Winston's wagging tongue, he had learned far more about his peers and their scullery maids than he cared to ever know. "I do absolutely know, but not as much as you. Do you see that meek woman acting the chaperone over there by the bench in front of Pelton House?" When his valet nodded, he went on. "Tell me about her."

Winston smiled quick and wide before sitting up and clearing his throat, pushing his glasses back into place. His moment to shine had arrived. "That, Your Grace, is the recently widowed Mrs. Harlow, fallen out of service with the Earl of Chadley, and newly employed within the Viscount Thomberton's household over in Hanover Square. There is quite the buzz about the state of her relationship with the earl and what she might or might not be carrying in her breadbasket—if you glean my meaning. Whispers are that the countess discovered them *in flagrante* and threatened to burn down the house if Mrs. Harlow wasn't removed from the premises immediately. The earl and the viscount are old friends, you see. It is believed a favor was called upon so that the earl could keep her nearby for... *reasons.*" Waggling his eyebrows suggestively before he continued, Winston appeared as smug and happy as a cat after eating a canary. "We shall see in a few months' time what is what."

"Impressive," Joss murmured, eyeing his valet with equal amounts wariness and respect. Bow Street would be hard-pressed to find a better informant.

"I don't know what it is!" Winston chortled merrily, his full cheeks dimpling with pleasure as he bloomed under the attention and approval. "But the ladies all talk to me. Always." His brown eyes went round, and he leaned forward over his crossed legs. "All. The. *Time.*"

"And that," Joss announced, "is why you are the man for the job."

"I shall not let you down, Your Grace." Chest puffed out with pride, Winston smoothed his features and inquired with calm focus, "What would you have me do?"

"Why, you're going to do what you do best. Gossip."

"Perfect!"

"Exactly." Joss tapped the tip of his nose and winked at his valet. "Now, you're going to do whatever mad magic you do and spread word that I will be in attendance at the Claremoore ball Saturday next. It's the biggest ball of the Season. An extravaganza, if you will. Everyone who is anyone will be there. So too will be Anonymous if they know I am attending. For these paintings always appear at a *ton* ball. That means that this *artist* has access to the highest realm of Society. And that means they are either a peer or a servant within the household of a peer. With your wildfire gossip, we shall uncover this culprit."

"What will you do once you're at the ball, Your Grace? How can you ensure this rapscallion will not evade you and reveal your humiliation anyway?"

Joss had not gotten that far. "Let me think upon it. I'll have it properly sorted before the ball." As he turned his attention once again out the front windows, his gaze snagged on shining copper-blonde curls peeking out from under a bonnet adorned with a wide lilac ribbon as two young ladies—one tall and stately and the other short and curvy—passed directly in front of his window on their way to Hyde Park. Instant recognition shot through Joss and scrambled his composure, sparking his irritation—like a cat petted against the grain of its fur. Suddenly his skin felt too tight, itchy. And his mood turned downright sour.

Nora Castlebury.

Joss grumbled under his breath about ill-tempered, poorly mannered chits and tore his gaze from the object of his irritation and her perfectly amiable sister.

"Do come up with a sound strategy," Winston urged, uncrossing his legs and rising from his chair, his brown eyes sobering. "Else your bare arse won't be the only thing exposed. Your theatre will be vulnerable too."

"Deuce it, Winston," Joss groaned, again raking a hand through his hair. "What did I tell you? Leave me well out of reason and reality."

"Yes, Your Grace."

There it was again. *The tone.*

"Oh, go gossip with the maids." Joss frowned and waved dismissively.

"Gladly." Winston chuckled and left the dining room with a bounce in his step and a whistle on his lips.

Joss had some rather intense scheming to do.

Chapter Two

Lady Nora Castlebury considered it a fine day for duplicitous planning.

The weather was warm, the sun was bright, the breeze was fragrant with blooms… and the Duke of Somerton was about to receive his comeuppance. Oh, what a wonderful day indeed. The very best.

"Serves him right for manhandling me," Nora muttered, her wonderful mood dampened momentarily by the memory of how rudely Rainville had tossed her over his shoulder and carried her from the Meadowlark Tavern that night several weeks ago. As if he had the right. Why, the unmitigated gall of the man! How it made her fume, the way men in general felt they owned everything and everyone. Women especially. He was no exception.

It was time to teach Joss Rainville, Duke of Somerton, a lesson.

"What has you smiling so smugly? I declare, you appear most mischievous!"

Swallowing her telling smile, Nora replied lightly, "Merely considering the myriad ways one can inflict extreme discomfort upon another without a single touch or word spoken."

"Well, that is rather concerning." Lottie, her youngest sibling, snorted indelicately and glanced down at her. "Though I undoubtedly should, I will refrain from inquiring further. Your mind is a mystery and, honestly, a tad frightening, dear sister."

"Ha!" Green eyes lighting with humor, Nora beamed up at Lottie as they strolled along Upper Brook Street on a lovely late June day, the skirts of her fine cotton walking dress flirting about her ankles. "That might be the nicest compliment you've ever paid me—thank you."

"It wasn't exactly a compliment, Nora," her sister drawled, casting her a wry side glance.

"And yet I took it as such anyway," Nora replied around a laugh, not at all offended. Linking her arm with Lottie, she leaned close and said, "I truly adore you."

"I adore you too," her sister replied with equal affection, her soft blue gaze sobering. "Although it still feels a bit odd promenading through Hyde Park without Carenza, don't you agree?"

"I do agree." Nora also missed their elder sister. "What's even more odd to me is addressing her now as the Viscountess of Amslee."

Passing by 32 Upper Brook Street, Nora clenched her jaw tight and refused to look at the magnificent five-story townhome with its warm yellow stone exterior and marble accents. To do so would prompt her to acknowledge the person who resided within its walls. And an arrogant, self-centered, overbearing duke was the last thing she wished to acknowledge. Nay, him she only wished to humiliate.

Unbidden, Nora's gaze slid left to the lush flowers flanking the stoop of the townhome's exquisite entrance, and she admired without thought the way they bloomed so colorfully, growing joyfully wild through the metal fence to brush against the pale marble pillars that held sentry over the ornately carved oak door. All those saturated hues against the pale stone backdrop! She swallowed her rising excitement, but her pulse quickened nevertheless as the artist in her longed for her brushes and canvas to render the scene into permanence.

Blast Rainville for possessing such an utterly decadent and charming front entrance.

"Do you think Carenza and Damon will be at the Claremoore ball next week?" Lottie inquired, her question turning Nora's attention from her great dislike of the man who resided within number 32—but not before she noticed a flash of rich, glossy gold behind the lavishly large bay window near the entrance door and caught sight of Rainville himself staring out at them, his hair glinting in the sunlight. The scowl on his countenance was hot enough to set the curtains beside him ablaze.

Taken aback, as she always was by the sheer physical beauty of the duke, Nora instinctively curled her gloved hands into fists, as a sudden, fiercely intense urge to sink her fingers into his lush, tawny locks washed over her. Her pulse skittered and she swallowed around the lump suddenly constricting her throat. "Deuce it all," she grumbled, deeply irritated at her reaction to Rainville's appearance. "That *gentleman* is a cad." To emphasize her words to herself, lest she forget because he was so blasted beautiful, she rotated her head and scowled directly back at the Duke of Somerton.

"I've no earthly notion as to what is happening right now, but I know you are most decidedly up to something, Nora." She could hear the lecture warming up in Lottie's tone. "It's impertinent, the way you are staring at His Grace just now. What is your possible motivation?"

Nora rolled her eyes in annoyance and returned her attention forward, noting the closeness of Park Street from the townhouse's front step. A fine location the duke enjoyed. Made her furious. Why did the most entitled of men also get to possess the most beautifully situated homes?

Truly, life was cruel.

Fortunately, Nora had a plan to even the scales some.

"You're not going to tell me what you're about, are you?" Lottie shook her head disapprovingly, and her wheat-toned hair fluttered about her quietly pretty face. "Shall I stop and inquire with the duke directly as to the nature of your ill regard for him? Perhaps he will be more forthcoming than you." Hooking a thumb over her shoulder at number 32 as they passed, Lottie smiled sweetly at her with the threat.

Knowing that Lottie was a most literal sort and would truly seek the duke out, Nora bit back the urge to stick her tongue out at the duke's home in a display of purely juvenile behavior and sighed instead, explaining, "Rainville behaved in a most ungentlemanly way several weeks ago, and I'm still quite enraged over it."

Lottie gasped, a gloved hand flying to the chest of her modestly styled printed blue walking dress, and she stopped and went still as stone on the bustling sidewalk near the corner of Park Street. "He didn't—"

"*No*, he did not." Not that. Never that. Rainville was arrogant and deserved a giant dose of humility, but Nora knew he would *never*.

Besides, the ladies came to him far too readily and willingly.

Oh, she had heard of his escapades. Heard the whispers. Opera singer, French widow, American heiress—Lord Bemberly's *wife*. The list went on.

"Then what, pray tell, did Rainville do to you that was so terrible? For he has never been anything but the perfect gentleman during our interactions."

They came to a stop at the intersection of Park and Upper Brook Street, Hyde Park gloriously lush and inviting just cross the way, beckoning to her. Squinting against the glare of sunlight reflecting off the glossy paint of a passing carriage, Nora looked up and down Park Street for their opening to cross. "If you must insist upon knowing," she huffed, annoyed at Lottie's insistent questioning, and nodded at the driver of a small hack as he brought his horse to a stop for the two of them to pass. She smiled at the young driver and took a step onto the hard-packed dirt road. "He saw me at a place *he* deemed unacceptable and bodily carried me from it like a… a *barbarian*," she blurted with a furious gesture of her hand. "As if he had the right!"

"That doesn't sound like the duke!" Lottie gasped again and glanced back over her shoulder, her blue bonnet ribbons dancing with the motion. "Are you certain you did not mistake his intention?"

"Trust me," Nora growled, latching on to her sister's wrist as Lottie gawked behind her at Rainville's townhouse. Tugging her across Park Street, she went on, "There was no mistaking his intentions or the blatantly offensive act of his tossing me over his shoulder. As if I was nothing more than a sack of flour. Not a human being with my own personhood, my own rights." Which were still *hers*, until she married. Carenza had taught her that.

"Oh my." Lottie's eyes grew round in surprise at the truth of Rainville's behavior.

"To add further insult..." Mollified somewhat by her sibling's reaction, once they reached the other side of Park Street and joined the flow of pedestrians meandering their way to the Grosvenor Gate entrance of the park, Nora continued, "The high-handed man threw me into his carriage and brought me home. Against my wishes."

"Oh," Lottie repeated, her gentle blue eyes round as dinner plates. "*Oh my.*"

"Precisely," Nora agreed in a clipped tone, anger sparking hot in her chest. "I've rather excellent reasons for disliking the Duke of Somerton."

"Did I hear someone speak my name?" called out a deep, amused voice from several feet behind them.

"*Noooooo,*" Nora groaned softly, curling her hands into fists as her step faltered. Squeezing her eyes tightly shut, she wished fervently for Rainville to just... well, just pass her by, or turn around, or perhaps disappear altogether. Every single interaction with the aristocrat ended poorly. Had he not learned by now they were best off not speaking at all to each other?

Besides, there was only so much pretending she could muster.

Pretend to smile.

Pretend to listen.

Pretend to *obey*.

Why must women surrender to the cage forced upon them by self-serving men who wanted the world to belong only to them? Too cowardly to share space with the female sex for fear they might be bested by something they wanted so desperately, that the power a woman alone held over them became an evil to squash—to own with total control. To want something and fear it with equal measure, when the obvious answer was simply to provide it respect and autonomy, room to breathe. That was men's burden that they laid upon themselves.

Poor, pitiful things.

"Not even a little," Nora grumbled at her own sarcasm, wanting to ignore Rainville.

Yet Society expressly forbade her from doing anything other than inhaling a steadying breath, squeezing her fists tight, and saying with false cheer through gritted teeth, "Your Grace," as the duke appeared beside her in his enormous, golden glory.

Lion-esque, the *ton* called the Duke of Somerton.

It pained her that she could not object to the descriptor.

Every shade from bronze to pale gold, Rainville's hair curled loosely about his head in casual disarray like a great lion's mane, ending in curls just above the collar of his jacket. And his eyes—such an unusual golden amber they were. Like rich clover honey dappled with bright, sunny citrine stone flecks. She could recall the exact shade of them with absolute clarity without even looking at him. Yet as unique—and yes, *lion-esque*—as his eyes were, it was the way the duke moved that had earned him the apt adjective. Powerful and prowling and graceful. Beauty and strength and grace wrapped up in one often arrogant, restless Duke of Somerton.

"Well, well, if it isn't the delightful Castlebury sisters! Lady Nora, Lady Lottie, how excellent to see you this fine day." Oh, Rainville said the words, but the *meaning* was so very different. He was as happy to see her as she was him.

Which meant he wasn't.

At all.

"Good day to you as well, Your Grace," Lottie seamlessly said, always so precise with things. It was a trait Nora wished she too possessed. Alas, she was a less organized, more chaotic sort of personality. "We only just walked past your townhome and were admiring your wonderful little front garden."

"Ah," Rainville murmured from entirely too close beside Nora. One of the largest men she had ever seen, the duke towered over her with his annoyingly broad, muscular shoulders, nearly casting her in complete shadow. "Then that is most certainly where I heard myself mentioned."

"Assuredly," Nora ground out in fake agreement, her jaw tight enough to crack. His very presence grated. Too much—it was too much. His presence dominated her senses.

"Excellent!" Rainville cheered, hands clasped behind his back as he continued to stroll along beside her, keeping pace easily when she quickened at Grosvenor Gate, eager to dash down one of the many offered paths and evade his unwanted company. "My sister, Claire, will be greatly pleased to hear of your admiration for the flowers, as she is the one responsible for the garden."

"How *is* your dear sister, Your Grace?" Lottie inquired, her face alight with genuine interest. "It has been ages since we have had the pleasure of her company!"

"Yes, I agree, it has been a rather long time." Smiling easily, blast him, Rainville simply oozed charm, and Lottie melted under it like butter in the hot sun, her cheeks blooming bright pink with pleasure. "However, she greatly prefers the quiet of our country estate, especially now that our parents have passed. The rolling fields and animals keep her well satisfied with their steady company. My horses, especially. I fear my mount has grown far too accustomed to sporting a braided and ribboned mane or tail."

"Your mount?" Nora's green eyes widened in surprise. "Do you mean that hulking beast with the abundant pastern feathering and head the size of a carriage wheel?"

Rainville laughed, his strange golden eyes lighting with delight as he looked down at her. "Oh, how Cinnamon Sticks would adore being described in such a way!"

Nora's eyebrows shot up in surprise. "That enormous horse is named *Cinnamon Sticks*?" A mighty creature suited to carrying knights of old and their weighty armor, the horse appeared far too intimidating to possess such a... *cute* name.

"He is indeed. Claire named him that when he was a mere foal, convinced his coat was the exact color of cinnamon."

"She's not wrong," Nora admitted, picturing the horse in her mind's eye. A rich brown coat with four white stockings and a bold white stripe down its face, it did in fact remind her of the spice.

"Pray tell, what breed is your mount, Your Grace? I've not seen one quite like him here in London," Lottie inquired as they continued their stroll, the duke now included in the promenade. Rather, he had included *himself*. And oh, how the good townspeople noticed as well, cutting them covert glances as they passed by and whispering feverishly to one another.

"Why, thank you for inquiring, my lady. I'm quite proud of his bloodlines, actually, as I've a keen interest in horse breeding, and Cinnamon Sticks is the result of a mare and stallion that I purchased from a farmer in the Lanarkshire region of Scotland. They are draft types known locally there as Clydesdales, and my mount was their first offspring."

"I had no idea you had such an interest," Nora murmured, glancing up at the duke.

"There is much about me you do not know," he replied lightly, almost dismissively, and she felt the small slight as if it were a full, blazing rejection. But then he latched on to her elbow and pulled her close to him, and her pulse skittered. "Beware the dog excrement."

Glancing down, Nora noted the smelly, fresh pile, and she would have landed a boot squarely in it if it had not been for Rainville's intervention. "Thank you," she begrudgingly offered, annoyed that he was behaving nicely. It made her plan harder to execute.

More precisely, it caused her conscience to whisper, to question her choice to execute it at all.

No. He deserved it. He did.

All men did.

Each man deserved it when she singled them out to learn a lesson in vulnerability, exposure. To know and experience the powerless life of *women*. To have choice taken away. To be objectified, mocked. To be made something less than a sacred being worthy of self-possession.

To be completely under the control and whim of another.

Her paintings of them in the nude forced the worst of the *ton's* men to live through a moment in time where something beyond their control, some*one*, dictated their life experience—and not only disrespected them but made them a spectacle to the world at large in the process. Such was the life of a woman. So, Nora flipped the page, took control back. For herself. For the little girls growing up under the inequity, the oppression. For ladies around the world forced into servitude in one fashion or another simply for possessing a sexual organ between their thighs that was coveted beyond measure by most men.

Nora sought justice for them all in her own secret way.

Bustling with pedestrians out enjoying the perfect London weather, the walking path suddenly felt far too constricting, far too public, for her liking. There was Lady Dutton and her three daughters over by the bench chatting animatedly with Lady Fennelwick. The group had most assuredly noticed Rainville accompanying her and her sister, for they kept staring while trying to pretend to do otherwise.

Oh, blast it all.

Nora stopped mid-stride and spun toward the golden behemoth in fancy peacock-blue velvet. Always the showman, that one, with his decadent styling. "Should you like something?" Tipping her head *way* back and squinting against the brilliant sun, she raised a brow in question at the duke. "Or are you here simply to make a nuisance of yourself?"

"Ceranora!" her sister gasped.

"It is quite all right, Lady Lottie," said a chuckling Rainville, and his amused reaction grated Nora's nerves entirely. "I take no offense, for your sister is quite the prickly hornet. I've learned to beware her stinger."

"I'll show you sting," Nora muttered, clenching her hands. But then she recalled all the curious eyes around them and forced a smile. "Such a marvelous sense of humor you possess, Your Grace."

"You believe that was a jest?" Rainville smirked down at her, and Nora had a flashing, fierce urge to kiss it right off his countenance.

This time, *she* gasped. At herself.

How could she *think* such a thing?

"Your Grace can have a good day." With that, she tipped her chin, spun on the heels of her favorite walking boots... and made it three steps before the duke stopped her with his words.

"Lady Nora, shall I see you at Claremoore's ball Saturday next?"

The color drained from Nora's face. Her stomach plummeted. Why was he inquiring? Her plan! She was to reveal the painting at the ball. Deuce it, did he *know*?

No, he couldn't. How could he? His knowing would be preposterous, ludicrous. Wouldn't it?

She would remain calm; he would not ruin her composure. "I suppose you shall, if you attend." Schooling her features into a serene mask and staring straight ahead, Nora waited for Lottie to reach her side before continuing, her heart thundering in her chest, "Enjoy your day, Your Grace."

Never, not ever before, had Rainville concerned himself with her presence at *any* event—other than his one vehement refusal of her right to enjoy a night out at the establishment of her choosing, in the London neighborhood of her choosing, when he had carried her over his shoulder from the Meadowlark Tavern. But certainly, he had never cared about a *ton* event.

Something tugged at her mind, and Nora slowed her pace once again and slid a glance over her shoulder. Rainville stood tall and powerful and bronzed—and her tongue stuck to the roof of her mouth and her throat went dry. How could one man possess so much masculine beauty? Especially a man she detested so verily. Life's cruelty, to be sure.

"Why do you ask whether I shall be there or not?"

Something passed behind the duke's eyes, a shadow that was present only for the briefest of flashes before disappearing, and a small, slightly mocking smile cupped his lips. "Perhaps I merely wished for more of your company, my lady."

Nora snorted. Inelegantly, and right there on the widest path in Hyde Park with members of the peerage mingling about and no doubt listening, she snorted. What else could she do at his blatant lie? "Perhaps you mistake me for a fool, Your Grace," she shot back.

"Or perhaps you mistake *me* for one," Rainville replied quietly, his golden gaze oddly intense and direct.

A shiver, cold and unnerving and threaded with foreboding, shot down her spine. "Lottie." Nora broke eye contact and notched her chin up as she addressed her sister. Her hands were not quite steady, so she fisted them once again. "Let us leave the duke to his undoubtedly busy schedule and continue our promenade. Good day, Your Grace."

Before he could reply, she latched once again on to her sister's arm and began marching down the park path and far away from the most infuriating man of her acquaintance.

Truly, he deserved what was coming to him.

Chapter Three

The trap was laid. Well, rather, the trap was laid as well as one could lay a trap. Joss deeply, profoundly hoped it worked. The success of his theatre depended upon his reputation remaining impeccable, unblemished to any degree. Perfect like that first white blanket of snow draping over the Somerset countryside.

Certain things affected a man's reputation; others did not. Enjoying the company of ladies did nothing to besmirch his Somerton name with investors, for a duke in his prime was expected to indulge in the benefits of his elevated station. No, his dalliances did not concern him. A nude painting of him did.

The scandal it would cause… Good God, the trouble! Joss could only imagine the headache. And his investors? Those silent pillars of financial support he sorely needed? Gone.

Having a foolhardy spendthrift for a father was an already glaring and permanent mark against him if that truth were to come to light, though thankfully no one knew aside from Winston—and most likely the entire household staff, because Winston's mouth flapped like a flag in the wind. However, tonight Joss could not fault him for it.

His valet's loose tongue was going to catch him an artist.

"You seem distracted tonight." Joss's companion pouted beautifully, her artful expression perfectly practiced, designed to inspire within him guilt and remorse for his inattentiveness. "Am I so uninteresting, Your Grace?"

His sometime lover, Lady Seraphina Lingbottom, wrapped her arm snug around his and pushed close, plumping her deep cleavage purposely against his bicep. Joss glanced down at her breasts, expecting the hum of arousal he had always felt in the past when she performed the motion. A sexually experienced woman of keen appetites, she loved nothing more than to insinuate sexual overtones into everything she did—especially in public. She adored the thrill of potentially getting caught.

Joss frowned, realizing he felt nothing at her overtures. Not a hum or a buzz or a tickle of interest. Not a single stirring in his loins. *Bloody excellent.*

What had come over him?

"Shall we find a more private place to continue our conversation, Your Grace?" This time Seraphina somehow moved in such a way that her breasts cradled his arm, squeezing him with her generous mounds. Slowly, ever so slightly, Seraphina lowered her body a fraction, and then straightened once again, stroking her breasts subtly against him. "Shouldn't you prefer something else between these?" she whispered suggestively.

Normally he would have. The widowed countess was a skilled and creative lover, physical perfection with her sable-colored eyes and dark hair such a striking contrast to her alabaster skin. Joss knew her nipples blushed dark rose when she was aroused.

Yet... nothing. Not a stir. Bloody concerning, that.

"Perhaps," he murmured for her ears only, "we should..." Joss trailed off, his attention turned by a flash of copper-blonde amongst the milling throng of brunettes and the occasional redhead. Only one woman possessed hair such a beautiful, unique color.

The acutely aggravating Lady Nora Castlebury. Intensely irritating. Feverishly frustrating. He could go on all day with alliterative terms describing the willful chit.

Alas, Joss had actual important business to tend to. Such as ferreting out a painting before his bare arse was shown to half of London.

Still, he noted, Nora's hair did look particularly appealing in the warmth of the candlelight tonight. Like the last flare of a Somerset sunset on a hot summer day. Or the first blush of passion.

Suddenly Joss felt the stirring, his desire awakening from its slumber. It unfurled its arms, stretched wide, and focused its attention. Only it wasn't on Lady Seraphina Lingbottom. Oh no, his blasted desire had to be much more contrary than that.

His desire was for *Nora*.

"Son of a b—" he swore, cutting himself off at the last second.

"Is everything all right, Your Grace?" Dark eyes met his, Lady Seraphina's lovely countenance full of concern. "Did I say something to upset you?"

"No," he rushed to say as a small bubble of panic rose in his chest. It could not be that infuriating chit his body responded to! His sexual appetite was more robust and less discriminating than that. Never before had it singled out a female as its sole focus of desire. Clearly, it was an oddity, a fluke.

Him wanting only Lady Nora Castlebury?

Please.

"I'm afraid I'm rather distracted by a personal matter this evening, my lady. Pray, do not be offended at my lack of attentiveness." He spoke the words, and yet his attention was in fact quite sharply focused—just not upon the countess.

Across the crowded ballroom, Lady Nora laughed, her smile open and without artifice, and his gaze swooped like a hawk to the exposed column of her throat, so graceful and damnably kissable. Any bloody dandy could plant their lips upon that vulnerable flesh if they chose. Did she not have other dresses? Ones less... pretty?

Why did he care about Lady Nora Castlebury's potential suitors? The woman was wasp-tongued and far too opinionated for his liking. What did he care if some poor bloke decided to saddle himself with that baggage?

"I bloody don't," Joss grumbled, and internally shook himself, dragging his attention from the infernal Castlebury woman. He refused to acknowledge just how difficult a task that was.

A motion across the room near an alcove filled with lush potted plants gained his attention. At his advanced height he easily scanned the top of the crowd, finding the source of the motion. One of his footmen, Giles, motioned again. Joss nodded back. All exits were secure. If anyone left the ballroom or the Claremoore's house in any way, his men would take note, send him word, and follow. He was not letting Anonymous get away tonight.

Sweat beaded at Joss's temples, curling the hair there. Hotter than the West Indies in July, the ballroom barely breathed. Sconces and chandeliers dripped candles in excess, the expansive room shimmering in the abundant light as the *ton* milled about and mingled, cups of sparkling champagne punch in hand.

"Such a wonderous ball tonight, don't you think, Your Grace?" Lady Lingbottom inquired with a tilt of her head.

"Indeed it is, my lady." No peer would dare miss this night, this event. The Claremoore ball was the greatest mark of one's establishment within the peerage. To miss it was to cast one's next Season into the bucket of pariahs and social outcasts.

Anonymous would appear, Joss was certain of it. As certain he was that Lady Nora Castlebury was a thorn in his side. A spirited, gorgeous thorn.

"Your Grace, I am so pleased you are here this evening!"

Silently groaning, Joss braced himself and affected his countenance into perfect amiability. "Good evening, Lord Lambert. Excellent showing your mare put on at Chatterley Downs last Sunday. Loads of promise in that one."

"Why, thank you for such compliments, Your Grace." The smug, dark-haired marquess beamed and tugged at a black dress jacket sleeve. Average height and lean, Lambert did not look like much. Yet he was an expert fencer. More than once the marquess had displayed impressive skill while dueling at Otto's, a gentlemen's club of which they were both members. "I've high hopes for that one in the coming year." Eyes sharp and cunning, the marquess cut him a smile. "Come round after the races next time and I'll introduce you to her. I'm rather keen to discuss your theatre venture in detail, as well. Yes, do come by and we'll make a proper occasion of it."

"Sounds capital," Joss murmured, his attention quite distracted by the flashes of copper-blonde weaving through the crowded ballroom to the edges where Lady Nora stopped, and Joss watched as she craned her neck about as if searching for someone.

While that alone was cause for speculation, it was her expression that was most telling. Why, the lady appeared quite pleased with herself. Smug, even, if such a descriptor could be applied to a lady. Which, of course, it could.

Lady Nora Castlebury was smugness personified.

What, pray tell, had her in such a state?

Alarm bells ringing in his mind, Joss glanced about the crowded ballroom, noting the loosening laughter as the *ton* indulged freely in the renowned Claremoore champagne. Over the course of the last thirty minutes, the crowd had shifted from polite tones and subtle enjoyment to outright laughs and enthusiastic hand gestures. Between the steady flow of champagne and the musical quartet and the dancing, the attitude was greatly loosened from whence the ball began. Indeed, the *ton* was collectively inebriated. Distracted.

It was the perfect time to sneak in a ruinous nude painting without detection.

"If you'll excuse me?" Joss dipped his head in farewell to Lord Lambert. "I'm afraid there is something I must tend to." Lest Lambert become curious and wish to inquire further, he glanced pointedly down at his companion, the beautifully sulking Lady Lingbottom.

"Shall we, my lady?"

"Ah, I see how it is." The marquess clapped him on the back with a chuckle. "Go to it, man. Tend to your business."

Knowing that Lady Lingbottom suffered not at all for male companionship kept him from feeling guilty for what he was about to do. "Walk with me, my lady?"

"Of course," the countess purred, wrapping her gloved hands securely around his elbow and smiling coyly up at him. Her pale rose and gold-threaded gown rustled with her movements.

His gaze once again drawn to Nora, he nearly faltered when he noticed the glow of her skin underneath the chandelier lights, so delicate, so flawless. The exposed skin of her cleavage sent heat snaking through his belly.

Blast it, why?

Lady Nora was nothing but a headache. Best put him out of his misery now, if that was the direction his desire now aimed. Better to remind his body of the pleasures to be found with a variety of ladies, not simply one. He could start right now with Lady Lingbottom *and* position himself to better see what Lady Nora was up to.

With his instincts ringing in his ears, Joss drew the countess along the perimeter of the ballroom. The overpowering scent of flowers and expensive perfume combined clung to the fringe of the ballroom floor, and started his temples dully throbbing.

"I say, Your Grace, what have you in mind, leading me toward ballroom corners?" his companion whispered to him, her dark eyes boldly taking in his measurement. A slow, knowing smile spread across her full lips. "Perhaps I should have worn a different corset."

Joss returned her smile with his own, quick and sharp, scanning the crowded ballroom again—past lush and heavy brocade curtains, beyond the side tables overflowing with bouquets of exotic hothouse flowers, and through the sea of flushed and powdered *beau monde*—searching for Lady Nora. Like a string connected them, he found her, drawn by something invisible. A gut feeling, perhaps?

Precisely at that moment, like prey catching scent of a predator nearby, Lady Nora whipped her copper-blonde head around, and her gaze locked from across the ballroom with his. Locked and held as she tilted her chin at a defiant angle. Her shoulders, encased in exquisite silk of the creamiest, palest yellow, drew back, appearing taut as a bowstring as she stared him down.

Brazen chit.

Reluctant admiration stirred in his chest. Quite his misfortune that he generally admired such bold traits in a person. Yet, somehow, when possessed by one Lady Nora, their appeal changed considerably, became bloody aggravating.

"You truly are distracted this evening, Your Grace!" chided his companion. "Pray tell, what has your attention so firmly in its grip? For it is not me, that much is clear. Even if you are leading me somewhere for a tryst, I do not occupy your thoughts."

But she *does,* his mind whispered. And instantly, Lady Nora was there in his head, not only his vision. Beautiful and entirely too bold.

Joss growled under his breath, "No." With effort he broke eye contact and smiled down at his companion. "You are so lovely a visage, my lady, so captivating."

"Ha!" Lady Lingbottom tittered as he navigated them into a heavily curtained alcove, where a large potted palm plant obscured them from view. "Smooth-tongued devil. I know your game."

Truly, Lady Lingbottom didn't possess a clue what his true intent was. For Joss could now see, unobstructed from this vantage point, all the ballroom exits *and* a certain strawberry blonde. It niggled at him, the way Nora kept looking about, her attention stopping here and there upon those in attendance as if she were gauging their moods.

"Now, what did you wish to show me?" the countess purred against him, seeking his jaw line above his starched cravat, her lips finding purchase there. A distant part of him noted with dismay the lack of interested response on his part. "I confess I have missed your attentions," she added provocatively.

He had not, as it turned out, missed *hers*.

Taking Lady Lingbottom to the alcove had simply, in truth, been to obtain a better vantage point from which to observe the exits... and yes, also Lady Nora. His desire could not be stirred. "She's up to something," Joss muttered aloud, tilting his jaw away from the countess's affections. But she was like an octopus tentacle, suctioning her lips to him.

"Mmm?" Lady Lingbottom murmured in response as she pressed flush against him.

Gripping her elbows, Joss pried her from him as gently as he was able, but the countess held fast. "My lady, you'll leave marks."

"Is that such a terrible burden?" Lady Lingbottom cooed and nipped him with her teeth, scraping them lightly along his jaw.

Still, he felt nothing.

Suddenly, Joss noticed one of his men trying to gain his attention from across the ballroom. Raising a brow back in question, Joss tried again to pry the countess from his side, his golden gaze steady on his man, noting the direction he gestured. "I am a duke, my lady. It would be unseemly of me to bear such a mark."

"*Fine,*" Seraphina sighed gustily, lessening her attentions.

Following his man's direction, Joss cursed softly. "Damn it." Instantly on high alert, he watched as Lady Nora shared a covert glance with an unknown, passing servant, nodded once, and began to edge her way toward the far set of doors leading to the balcony. "What are you about?" he murmured.

"I am trying without success to engage your passions." Lady Lingbottom pouted and withdrew her lips from his jaw. "Whatever has your attention this eve is a formidable foe. One I clearly cannot win against." Stepping from him, the countess added, "I've too much pride to beg." Trailing a glove-covered finger down the center of his chest, she took another step in retreat. "You know where to find me when your head is once again clear."

Wary at the seemingly gracious retreat, and knowing the countess well enough, Joss held suspicion that she would seek retribution for any perceived slight in the future. But ultimately, he did not care. "Apologies," he offered. "My mind is restless this night."

"Now your body will be also." With a smirk cupping her lips and her dark eyes flashing, Lady Lingbottom ran a finger over the front of his trousers and disappeared from the alcove in a swirl of pale rose silk.

"Might regret that," Joss mused aloud, already forgetting her, sharply focusing his gaze across the room on a certain Castlebury stealthily slinking her way to the balcony doors. With each group she passed, Nora mimicked their behavior, blending in unnoticed. Like a chameleon.

She was brilliant.

Clever.

Subtle, too, as she slipped seamlessly out the cracked balcony doors.

He should have known. "Of course it's her." It made perfect sense if he thought about it. And thinking about it gave him feelings. Big, angry, how-dare-she feelings.

With emotions rising rapidly in his chest, Joss signaled his man to remain behind and moved from the alcove, intent on following Nora. He took several steps, searching the ballroom to note if anyone else behaved irregularly, noting briefly that Lady Lingbottom had already replaced his company with a young buck in too-tight trousers. *Good.* Saved him a headache.

Moving through the crowd with the grace of a predator, Joss made his way to the double doors and silently slipped through, breathing thankfully the fresh night air. Ballroom air was positively stifling.

"Where did you go, minx?" Scanning the stone balcony and the dozen or so people milling about, Joss found his frown deepening when he did not immediately see Lady Nora. Searching past the balcony into the night, he was about to curse in frustration when he spotted a flash of pale silk move through the garden and disappear behind a tall, decorative hedge.

"There you are." Taking the balcony steps two at a time, the tails of his black dress jacket flapping gently behind him, Joss gritted his teeth and set off into the moonlit garden after her. "Reckless, headstrong girl," he growled as he stalked through the lush, fragrant back garden of Claremoore House. Gravel crunched softly underfoot as he strode down the path. "What is she thinking?" The blasted woman was either out in the garden for a tryst or she was quite possibly the elusive culprit he'd set out to catch. It was unclear which possibility he preferred.

"Neither," he spat, coming around a sharp corner in the topiary.

And there she was.

Lady Nora Castlebury, gorgeous as anything in her pale silk gown, the full moon illuminating her in silvery, ethereal light. A look of utter shock and dismay was frozen upon her countenance as she clutched a large, unframed painting in her sneaky, lying little hands.

Joss rolled to a stop and leisurely drawled, "Well, well, well, what have we here?"

"Your Grace!" she cried weakly, and hid the canvas behind her back. Her eyes were huge, dark pools in the moonlight. "You startled me! I did not hear you coming. I am merely out for a stroll. Some fresh air, you see," she stammered, clearly flustered.

How dare she?

How dare she?

"Save it," Joss sneered as anger sparked hot and wild inside him. He prowled to her, his long, powerful strides eating up the ground. When she retreated, he simply followed until she came to an abrupt stop against the topiary hedge.

"Your Grace," she pleaded, but he was deaf to her.

Instead, Joss leaned down until his nose was nearly touching hers. "Lady Nora," he growled, close enough to her that he could feel the warmth of her breath, and he snaked a hand around behind her back. Latching on to the unframed canvas and snatching it free, Joss growled with open menace, "Or should I say, *Anonymous?*"

Chapter Four

Panic sliced through Nora, splitting her in two. One part of her wanted to grab the painting back, toss it into the tall hedge behind her, and pretend innocence. The other part—the part that, more often than not, got her in heaps of trouble—wanted to claw and hiss and fight. She was not *wrong* for believing men's privilege was beyond the pale, beyond all acceptability.

And she was not wrong, as a woman, for *doing* something about it.

Defiance sparked, straightening her spine, and she met Rainville's anger with her own. "Get out of my space, *Your Grace*. It is a courtesy I have not bestowed upon you. Nor will I ever," Nora said, releasing her hands from behind her back to shove against the enormous duke's infuriatingly solid chest. "Why won't you *move*?" She grunted, shoving with all her might.

"You think you can handle me?" Rainville raised a haughty, bronzed brow at her. "I think not."

"You handled *me*." And the fury of it still burned in her chest. Tears stung the backs of her eyes, tightened her throat. "You had no right." Her voice cracked.

It was terrifying, what men felt entitled to do.

"What I did," the duke snarled, still far too close for her liking, "was save your reputation." His breath washed hot across the exposed skin of her neck. "Had you been discovered, your entire family would be in ruins by now."

"Well, how very gallant of you." Nora's voice dripped false sweetness.

"Actually, it was," he said, anger nearly melting his words.

"I did not *ask* for your interference!" she shot back, reaching around the giant jerk as he had done earlier, seeking the painting.

"Too slow." Rainville smirked and raised his arm well above his head, removing the painting from her reach, taunting her like a childish bully. Even jumping, she could not get to it now.

"*Oooooh!*" Anger flaring wildly, Nora lost her self-possession and reacted blindly. "Give that back!" In one motion, she stomped down furiously on the duke's Hessian, and then leapt high, using his muscular shoulder for leverage as she grabbed for her painting above their heads.

Rainville's surprised grunt felt supremely satisfying. "You little vixen!" Swearing a streak of profanity more suited for dockworkers than a duke, he wrestled her briefly and won.

"Damnation," Nora panted, her heart thundering from the exertion. "Why are you so blasted large?"

"Why are you so intent on ruining me?" The words sliced through the night.

She refused to dignify his question with an answer. "Why do you believe you can make decisions for a woman you hold no claim over?"

Rainville narrowed his eyes. "What do you mean?"

"I'm referring to me!" Nora exploded, shoving his chest again, to no avail. She might as well be an ant for all the good it did. "The way you manhandled *me!*"

"Beg your pardon? I did no such thing." Good gravy, he sounded offended. *Offended.* When it was *he* who threw *her* over *his* shoulder, not the other way around.

Suddenly feeling quite hemmed in and cornered, Nora tried to slide left and away, but he simply caged her in with his arms, one on each side of her head like steel bars, the painting still in his hand and pushing into the hedge. Defiance reared, and she slapped at his forearm. "You, sirrah, are a *bully*."

This time the duke smiled, cold as ice. "It takes one to know one, *Anonymous*."

"I'm no bully!" Nora gasped and slapped at his forearm again. "Move this appendage immediately." She even utilized her sternest voice. Did he move his arm?

No.

No, he did not. *Bully*.

"I'm quite through with this conversation," Nora announced, using her haughtiest tone.

"Oh, I'm only beginning." The promise in Rainville's tone sent chills down her spine. "You're going to tell me what your aim is with this painting." He shook it in his fist, rattled the canvas next to her head.

"And if I don't?" Nora tipped her chin defiantly, noting the full, glowing moon overhead.

"Oh, but you will," Rainville snarled, his eyes flashing in the moonlight.

"But I won't."

"Yes, you will."

"No, I won't."

"*Nora*," the duke growled in warning.

"*Rainville*," she spat right back, eyeing the canvas next to her head and contemplating how she might best retrieve it from his grip.

"Christ, you're aggravating."

This she already knew. "Not nearly so aggravating as *you*."

Suddenly the duke made a low, rumbling, warning sound that started in his chest and seemed to build and resonate out into the balmy night air.

"If you're trying to intimidate me," she blustered, "it's not working."

It was absolutely working.

"You know," the duke suddenly mused, altering his tone, turning contemplative as he shifted a boot-covered foot and relaxed his shoulders some. "If you had wished to gain my attention, there are other ways to go about it."

Lightning struck, right in her stomach, and Nora jolted. "*Excuse me?*"

"It's the only possible explanation for your painting."

Well now, that was beyond insulting. She slapped his forearm again as tears blurred her vision. Oh, how angry he made her! "It's *not* the only reason!" Nora shouted, suddenly quite overwhelmed at the state of her life's experience. Women were told what to do, when to do it, and how to do it. And, by goodness, women were told their very own feelings and motivations by another—by a *man*. As if women could not possess a thought or feeling that was not expressly chosen by them. "How could you, a *man*, know anything at all about what I'm truly feeling?" Nora shook her head. "You cannot. All you may do is *dictate* what you believe I should feel and think. What you believe I *am* thinking and feeling. But you do not have a clue, not an inkling. All you possess is arrogance and a superior attitude."

"Ah, is that the way of it?" His tone changed again, softened a degree.

Nora was not fooled. "Yes, that is absolutely the way of it! You march in here all fancy with your title and your clothing and your privileged male status, and *you*"—she reached for the painting shoved into the topiary near her head, but he yanked it away—"start making decisions and ascribing feelings and actions upon us."

"Us?" the duke inquired quietly, his face and body still far too close for her liking. His presence was too big, too male, too... Well, just too everything.

"Yes, *us.* Women, you dolt." Was her sex that easy to dismiss and forget?

"Methinks you protest much, my lady." This time a ghost of a smile crept over his lips; their finely sculpted beauty was illuminated in the glimmering moonlight. "Why is that?"

"Because I am fed up with men!" Nora shouted, losing her temper. "All of you!" She shoved against his chest again, this time blind to her own motions. Caught off guard, he rocked back on the heels of his boots and loosened his grip on the painting. It slipped from his fingers and landed on the clipped garden grass with a muffled thump. "Every single one of you thinking you can determine a woman's life for her, determine her thoughts and feelings and wants! You *can't*. I'm so sick of the way men flaunt themselves, the way they keep women on leading strings. None of you know anything of what it's like to be us! All you bloody well know is that you wish to control us. Not understand, not respect, not listen to us. Just *control*."

Rainville stood quiet for a moment, seemingly stunned by her outburst. "So, your response is that you paint humiliating images of the men of the *ton* and publicly display them? For what? Enjoyment? Embarrassment?" he demanded to know, his gaze intense and steady on her.

"To show the worst offenders what it's like!" Nora cried out, the injustice overwhelming her. She swooped down and snatched the canvas, then bundled it protectively against her chest as emotions swept over her, mindless to which side of the painting was pointed out toward the duke.

"Show them what what's like?" Rainville narrowed his eyes. "To be naked in public?"

"Yes!" Nora exploded. "Damn it, yes! To be powerless and vulnerable and at the mercy and whim of another. Women endure it every single day of their lives!"

"Women also enjoy a certain level of comfort in their daily lives, I'd wager," the duke returned, tall and fit and tense as he stood before her.

"Well," she bit off, snapping her spine straight. "That is rather ripe of you to say. You, who has enjoyed the most extreme luxury and comfort of us all, *Duke.*"

"Is that why you did it?" His deep voice was quiet, unsettlingly so, as he took a step toward her. She loathed the way he moved, so graceful and dynamic. Like a cheetah. Before she knew what he was about, he grabbed the canvas once again from her grip. "You seek to humiliate me because I have known the benefits of a monied life?"

"Because you believe yourself entitled above everyone else! Because you believe yourself above reproach. Because you believe you can choose and dictate for *me*! That's why I did it. Only *I*"—Nora thumped her chest with a gloved fist, feeling the fire of her conviction burn hot behind her ribcage—"get to do that."

"Let us see the havoc you thought to wreak upon my life, shall we?" Rainville said, his tone suddenly conversational, as if he were discussing biscuits and tea.

Pressure squeezed Nora's chest tight, and she cried out, "No!" suddenly not wanting him to see what she had done.

Angling the painting so that it was illuminated by the moonlight, Rainville released a long, low whistle as he stared down at the canvas. "Impressive," he murmured.

So many feelings flooded her at once. Self-consciousness, defiance, rebellion, and too many others. They swarmed her like bees to a hive of honey. "I—"

"No, no, don't interrupt," he scolded. "I'm studying a painting."

Nora fought the urge to roll her eyes and huff. "I—"

Rainville raised a finger to his lips. "Shh."

Nerves leaping along her skin and through her belly like frogs after a rainstorm, Nora felt the scream building inside, and clenched her jaw tightly. Something about the way he assessed the painting had her breath hitching, her heart beating a rapid drum in her chest. Nerves of another kind began to snake slowly through her belly.

Several moments passed before he lowered the painting and turned his attention to her. "You believed this would teach me a lesson, did you?"

Swallowing around her nerves, Nora straightened her shoulders and replied with as much defiance as she could muster, "Absolutely."

"I think you perhaps should look at your painting again." Now his voice sounded odd—Nora detected a husky note that had not previously been present. And his stance had changed, relaxed, loosened. Why?

"I know what my painting looks like," Nora snapped, crossing her arms defensively over her chest and glancing about the late-night summer garden, noting the abundant flowers flanking the garden paths. With the full moon above and the balmy breeze, it appeared quite the beautiful night to be strolling about the garden.

Unfortunately, she was with *him*. And nervous. Why was she so blasted nervous?

"Why should I look at a painting that I myself made?" Nora knew what was there. Rainville nude and lounging back on his elbows, one leg raised, his genitalia on display. The duke was smiling at his gawkers, a half-circle of ladies openly assessing the duke's appearance, their expressions ranging from curiosity to disdain to mockery to leering. And he—well, he was completely oblivious to it all, like a fool. "I know what I was feeling, what I was thinking. What I composed."

"Do you?" Rainville asked, his voice taking on a rough edge as he turned the painting toward her. "Because this teaches me something, all right, but it is not the lesson you think."

Nora glanced down at her painting and quickly looked away, tightening her arms over her chest. "It's exactly what I knew would be there. You, naked as a spectacle while women mock and belittle you." Exactly as all her paintings. Women mocked the naked men. Because every day in Society men mocked and ogled women.

"Look again," he urged, holding the painting closer and tipping it to catch the moon's reflection. "You've another secret you've been keeping."

Alarm flashed through her, and Nora glared and grabbed at the painting. "I do not have any other secret." What in the devil was he talking about?

"Oh, but you do." The way he said it had chills of a whole different sort darting down her spine. Suddenly, *quite* suddenly, it was rather difficult to breathe.

Rainville loomed over her, large and strong and beautiful and utterly spoiled and abhorrent. "You are imagining whatever it is you believe you see there." He was. Because there was nothing there that she had not painted. And she knew well what she had painted.

"But I'm not." Somehow his voice kept making her pulse skitter. It was too warm, too familiar in tone. Too... alluring. "For goodness' sake, let me see." Just to prove him wrong. Only that reason. Not because his insistence had a niggling bit of doubt creeping into her mind.

Leaning forward to better catch the moon's light upon the canvas, Nora did not realize how close she was to the duke until his scent permeated her nostrils. Leather and sunshine and a hint of sandalwood. She breathed deep. Of *course* he would smell good. "I see nothing, no secret."

"It's there," Rainville murmured. "You've been watching me very closely, haven't you?"

Her stomach fluttered. "No more than anyone else I wish to paint."

"The artist's eye, then?" His words skimmed over her cheek, caressed her neck.

"Yes." All subjects were carefully studied for exact execution with the brush. The duke was no exception.

Suddenly Rainville was close enough that his broad chest brushed against her shoulder. "That's how you so accurately depicted the size of my co—"

"Yes!" Nora squeaked, cutting him off as heat flooded her cheeks.

"Ah," Rainville replied, his tone gently mocking. "Tsk, tsk, Lady Nora. Don't you know it's impolite to stare at a man's co—"

"*Stop* saying that word!"

A low laugh rumbled in his chest, irritating her. He was clearly enjoying her discomfort. *Bully.*

"What of the women in this painting?" His low tone felt like physical touch. How indecent.

"They're gawking," she replied. Nothing more, nothing less.

"They're not just gawking, and it's not *women*. It's one woman. I think you've been keeping many secrets, my lady."

Panic unfurled and threaded through Nora's veins. What on earth was the duke talking about? She had no other secret. "They're just random, made-up women," she insisted.

"They're *you*," he claimed.

Nora gasped. "You lie!" She bent low to examine the women's painted faces, and her heart nearly exploded when she peered close and saw her own face reflected back at her. Different hair colors, different eye colors, but same face. Rainville was right. It was her. "I... I didn't know." Her lips felt numb from shock.

"Nora." His voice was close to her ear now, and the warmth of his breath made her shiver in a strange, exciting way.

She glanced up at him, her eyes huge as she absorbed the truth. It was her face she'd painted staring at Rainville. And the expressions she had made upon her faces weren't derisive, weren't mocking. They were *hungry*.

"I—" she started.

"*Want me,*" Rainville whispered hotly. "You bloody well want me, minx."

"I—"

Her, want the duke? *Yes,* something inside her whispered. *Yes.*

Shocked, Nora made a helpless, small sound.

Rainville took her mouth. One moment he was looming over her, big and smelling good and far too arrogant, and then he was claiming her with a kiss unlike any she had ever experienced before. Not chaste like the previous two she had received from overeager suitors. No, Rainville kissed her in a half-feral sort of way, with teeth and tongue… Oh, his tongue. It dueled deliciously with hers in a dance that set her blood sparking.

Flooded with heat, Nora dropped the painting to the ground and threw her arms around Rainville's neck, meeting his kiss with abandon.

"Damn it all, you taste good," he growled against her lips, pulling her flush against his large, hard body and taking her in another extraordinary kiss.

"I despise you," Nora panted when they separated, her body pliant against his, betraying her words.

"And I despise you." His large, strong hands stroked boldly down her body, cupped her backside. He squeezed, and she released a tiny moan of pleasure. "But you like that." He kissed her jawline, nibbled his way to her ear. "And I like it too."

"Don't say such things," she protested weakly, her body overheating at his confession.

"Then you should not have painted yourself watching me work my cock, minx. For now I know your secret fantasy, and it will fuel mine from here forward. Tell me," he growled as his hands raced up her ribcage to cup her full breasts. "Did you touch yourself when you imagined my naked body?"

A whimper escaped Nora and her head fell back, exposing the column of her throat. Oh, his wicked hands. So delicious. When they were on her she lost all thought, all rationality. *Damn him.*

"Did you?" he asked again, brushing his thumbs over her nipples, puckering them tight with arousal. "Did you slip your hand between your thighs?"

She gasped as desire flared at his crude words. Could she? Could she be bold enough to answer?

"Yes," Nora whispered.

"*Christ,*" he breathed. "Now you've done it."

And his mouth was on hers again, feeding her kisses of such heady passion that she lost all sense of anything but the feel of him.

"I tell you there was a woman in distress behind this hedge. We must see if she is in trou—"

"Oh!"

"Goodness!"

Nora froze as the voices filtered through the fuzz in her mind.

"Ah, hell," Rainville swore under his breath, then slowly straightened from her and turned to look at the sudden crowd. "Lady Lingbottom," he drawled, a hard note underlying his voice. "Everyone else."

"Care to explain yourself, Your Grace?"

Nora recognized her father's icy voice, and dread pooled heavy in the pit of her belly. *Oh no. Oh no, oh no.*

"Not especially," the duke replied, his tone deceptively light. Interesting that he did not push away from her. Instead, he held steady by her side. "Private moment and all."

"Then there is nothing to discuss, and I shall see you at our meeting first thing tomorrow morning," her father stated with frosty detachment.

A meeting? What meeting? Why did her father and Rainville need to meet?

Oh, but Nora knew. And she hated it with all her being.

They were meeting to discuss the terms of the *wedding.*

CHAPTER FIVE

"Fifty thousand."

Joss assessed the Earl of Castlebury as he stood beside an ornate wooden desk in the aristocrat's study at Tipton House, the grandest home in all Mayfair. "That is not enough." For him to marry Nora Castlebury, the earl needed to do better. "Your daughter was set to ruin me."

"Therefore, you ruined her first?" Wiping a hand over his thick white mustache, Nora's father sized up Joss with shrewd, cold eyes. "Bad form, son."

"It's Your Grace." No matter that he should not have kissed the infuriating chit, Joss refused to be demeaned by an aristocrat he outranked. "And it was not an intentional ruination."

"Oh, well, that makes it all rather fine, then, doesn't it?" Castlebury clipped the tip of a cigar, clamped it between his teeth, and lit the tip. "Do you take me for a fool, *Your Grace*?"

"Not at all, *my lord*. I know you to be an excellent businessman and strategist." Which was exactly why Joss had scooped Lady Nora up at the Meadowlark before her irascible behavior could tarnish the earl's reputation. Lord Castlebury was high on his list of potential investors. Ancient title, deep pockets, and a keen interest in new business ventures. Of course Joss would approach him. Now seemed a rather excellent time, all things considered. Though he truly had no choice but to marry Nora, he could leverage as much as he possibly could in the bargaining.

He did have an impoverished dukedom to consider, after all.

Though his gut burned at the thought of marriage to anyone, let alone the most aggravating woman of his experience, Joss could not in good conscience refuse to do what was right. If for no other reason than to be different than his father. Destroying a young woman's future and tarnishing the reputation of her entire family's name would not have slowed the former Duke of Somerton for even a moment. The duke and only the duke had mattered.

Him and parties. And gambling. The duchess had come a distant fourth in George Rainville's life.

Joss had not even ranked in the top ten.

"Tell me, Castlebury, what would you have done in my situation? Your daughter is utterly frustrating and defiant and... beautiful. What would you have done if, say, you had discovered a desirable woman with a scandalous, arousing painting in her grip? A painting of *you*. And you suddenly realized her innocent desire? And you were alone and there was moonlight and fragrant flowers and a titillating argument that stirred the senses?" Joss raked a hand through his thick golden tresses and swore. "Deuce it, your daughter is a force of nature."

The room fell silent before the earl released a long, *long* sigh. His pale blue eyes thawed just the tiniest degree. "First Carenza, and now this. I tell you, Duke, these girls are going to be the death of me."

"I believe you." Joss inhaled deep and scanned the luxurious study for the sidebar. He needed a drink. "Care to share a brandy?" He found it behind the desk, and strode on long, powerful legs to it. "May I?" he asked, gesturing to the bottles of spirits.

"Make mine a double whisky," the earl replied, an uncharacteristic hint of weariness in his tone. Turning, he found his desk chair and sank into it, rubbing the heel of a palm against his chest. His ample waist stretched the buttons tight across his black dress jacket. "It's been a damned day."

"Tell me about it," Joss muttered, and relaxed a hip as he poured the two of them glasses. Him, married to Nora Castlebury. *Bloody hell.* "I have to marry your daughter."

"Norabell's not so bad once you get past her bluster," the Earl of Castlebury said, accepting the offered glass with a tip of his chin.

Norabell?

"Clearly you jest," Joss scoffed before taking a deep drink of mighty fine brandy. "Excellent. Is this locally made?"

"Actually, it is." The earl brightened, sitting up a little in his overstuffed leather chair. "I've an interest in a distillery out just past the west edge of the city in the tiny village of Lipton. Pop in if you ever pass through and they'll give you a tour of the facilities. Fascinating process, really."

Ah, business ventures. The perfect topic. "I'll be certain to do just that. Mind if I…?" Joss gestured with languid grace at the chair directly across from the earl.

"Not at all—take a seat." Castlebury set his cut crystal snifter on the glossy surface of his desk with a slight click. "We might as well be comfortable while we tussle over the terms of this marriage agreement and Nora's dowry."

Settling into the deep cushions of the chair, Joss nodded. "I don't know about you, but I would rather this be a civil affair."

"Agreed. Having three daughters is headache enough. So much fuss they bring. *So much fuss.* Should you be blessed with daughters of your own, you'll understand. I offer my condolences in advance."

The thought of children had Joss blanching. "Look," he started, crossing a booted foot across his knee and settling in comfortably. "We both know this was an accident."

"Accident or not, Duke, you're obligated to marry her now. Besides, lips don't simply fall upon another's by mistake, no matter how tempting they are. It is a decision. With consequences." Castlebury slowly swirled the amber whisky in his glass and offered a small, unsympathetic smile. "This is yours."

Anger brewed in his gut, but Joss held steady, remained calm. "So you keep pointing out." He raised his glass of brandy, took a sip.

"If I have to force my favorite daughter into marriage, there are worse societal connections than to a duke," the earl admitted, leaning back in his desk chair. "I will use it to my advantage."

"Ah, but not before I use this unfortunate situation to *my* advantage." Joss uncrossed his leg, leaned forward, elbows on knees, and leveled his golden gaze on the earl. "Your daughter had a painting. Of me. *Nude*. With the sole intent and purpose of humiliating me."

"I knew I should never have allowed that French art tutor into this house!" Castlebury grumbled with a shake of his head. "Nothing but trouble." Suddenly his eyes narrowed on Joss. "Wait, are you suggesting that my Nora is the one behind the lurid paintings I've heard are sweeping the *ton*?"

"That is precisely what I am saying." And it still galled that she was willing to ruin him that way. "Your daughter has been very naughty, my lord."

"Deuce it! Does anyone else know about this?"

Joss shook his head. "Not that I'm aware. I hid the painting in the garden hedge and had one of my men collect it after the crowd dispersed."

Castlebury blew out a breath. "Well, that changes the situation a bit." He brushed a hand across his mustache again and scowled. "It seems I've two scandals in one with that girl." As he spoke, his face began to blotch and turn an unflattering shade of red. "Damn her!" A meaty hand curled into a fist and thumped angrily against the desktop.

Unease skimmed up the back of his neck as Joss took another slow sip, watching the earl struggle with his temper. This was a side to Castlebury he had not yet seen. One that was less than flattering. Nora's furious words from earlier sprang to his mind, and he saw it, understood the seed of her outrage. It had most assuredly sprouted from her own father.

"All right, Duke, it seems I have a rather large scandal to avert and have lost any bargaining power I may have possessed. Stupid girl, causing such grief. What are your terms?" The resignation in the earl's tone was underscored by a hard note of fury.

His terms. How Joss loved those two little words. "You are aware that I own Rhodes Theatre on Tavistock Street in the Garden District."

"I know you purchased it last year, yes." The Earl of Castlebury dragged slowly on his fat cigar. "You had me there weeks ago when Carenza sang. Nice place, though a bit of a gamble, don't you think, situated as it is so near Drury Lane and the Royal Opera House?"

Joss smirked. "Not when you've obtained the best playwright London has seen in a hundred years."

"You landed Thatcher Goodrich?" The earl raised a bushy white brow in surprise.

"The very one." And it pleased Joss to no end, though the deed was not completely done. Compensation still needed to be settled upon.

"I heard it said that King William favors him. Having him as your writer in residence will be quite the boon."

"It will, won't it?" Joss said, and straightened, leaning back once again in his chair. "Genius such as Goodrich's does not come cheap, however. Neither does maintaining an entertainment venue as grand at Rhodes. Having an investor with clout and reach in both the business and social worlds could be greatly beneficial," he ended with a pointed look at the earl.

"So you say," murmured Castlebury, puffing on the cigar. "And if you had such investors?"

"I would settle for long-term investment in Rhodes and forty thousand."

For several tense heartbeats the earl stared at Joss with unreadable ice-blue eyes. "She had a portrait of you, you say?"

"Of my very naked form, yes." Joss nodded. Given the current company, he pushed the image from his mind. Thinking of Nora's highly erotic painting while sitting across from her father was not a position he relished being in.

"Anatomically correct?"

Joss nodded again. "Yes."

"Hell's bells." Heavy, deep sigh. Then Castlebury raised his mostly empty snifter in grim salute. "I guess there's nothing left to say but welcome to the family, son."

<hr />

"WHAT WERE YOU thinking, Nora?" Lady Castlebury shouted, and threw her hands up in dismay. "What on earth were you *possibly* thinking?" Waving her hands wildly about her, the countess frantically paced across the plush plum-colored rug in Nora's bedchamber.

"She was probably thinking that the duke could kiss rather well, I'd wager," Lottie answered with a wry half-smile. "If she was thinking anything at all, that is."

"Thank you for that, Carlotta," Nora drawled, shooting her younger sister an unamused glance.

"You're welcome." Lottie chuckled, her blue eyes lit with levity and humor. "I am impressed, actually, for I doubt I would be thinking anything at all if Rainville were to kiss *me*."

A feeling, hot and possessive, shot through the pit of Nora's stomach, and she snapped, flinging herself back onto her oversized bed. "But he did *not* kiss you."

"True, unfortunately." Lottie sighed wistfully and winked.

"I knew you possessed a keen interest in him!" Nora hissed, and rolled her head to the side to glare at her sister.

"He *is* rather pretty," offered Carenza as she stood at the large double windows overlooking the dark back garden of Tipton House.

"You're here for moral support, Car. Not to make this terrible, awful situation worse." Nora hefted herself up onto her elbows, rustling her silk ball gown with the movement.

"You did that well enough by yourself," snapped Lady Castlebury. Stopping directly in front of Nora, she added, "Though trapping a duke into marriage is rather brilliant, I must admit."

"It was not on purpose!" Nora protested as her heart thumped heavy behind her ribs. "And it never would have happened at all if I had known Lottie wished him for herself."

"I don't wish him for myself," her youngest sister replied with a shake of her head. "I was merely trying to lighten the seriousness of the moment. Not that Rainville isn't pretty, mind you, because he is. But it's his interest in theatre that intrigues me most."

"Then *you* marry him," Nora grumbled, swinging her feet over the side of her four-poster bed and coming to a stand. "I don't want him."

"You should have considered that before you kissed him in the garden at Claremoore House!" Lady Castlebury barked with a hand pressed dramatically to her forehead as she continued to pace. "There is absolutely nothing to do now but marry the duke and save us all from ruination."

"What if he doesn't want to marry me?" The words shot out before Nora knew it was a thought she even possessed. "What if he refuses?" Her nerves spiked at the thought.

"Rainville won't do that," Carenza replied with calm certainty, her bright blue eyes steady as she turned her attention from the window. "Trust me. I know that he will do the right thing by you."

Nora scoffed and wrapped her arms around herself, hugging tight as emotions poured through her, sent her careening off balance. "You don't know him like I do."

"True," Carenza replied lightly. "I know him better."

Though she wanted to argue with her sister, Nora could not. It was true that Carenza knew the duke quite well from her secret life as the famous London tavern singer, the Masked Meadowlark. For months Rainville had pursued her to perform in his theatre, and she had finally agreed. Her first performance there had been extraordinary. "Did you agree with his new idea?" she demanded to know, feeling quite suddenly as if everyone else in the world knew this man that she must marry far better that she did herself. The sensation rankled and unsettled her greatly.

"What idea?" Lottie chimed in from her spot on the bed. The tip of her long, wheat-colored plait brushed the amethyst-toned bedcover.

"I am still considering it," Carenza replied, ignoring Lottie's inquiry as she brushed a sunny blonde curl from her cheek. "It is an ongoing discussion I've been having with Damon."

"Where is your husband?" Lady Castlebury demanded, looking frazzled and haggard. "He should be here during such a crisis."

"As should Crawford and Catamount," Lottie pointed out. "As the heir and heir presumptive of this family, they should be here to help mitigate the damage this scandal could cause." The youngest Castlebury pretended to look around for her brothers. "Yet I do not see them. Where are *they*?"

"Tending to important business, I'm quite sure," Lady Castlebury hastened to say. "Catamount rarely has a moment away from his duties at Bow Street with his Runners, and Crawford is busy learning the details of your father's shipping business, as well as the expected roles and duties of being the next earl. It is unreasonable to expect them to be so readily available to us."

"I think it is a rather reasonable expectation in a circumstance like this," Nora argued, anger at the whole situation burning hot in her chest.

"Damon is downstairs, Mother." Carenza's quiet voice cut through the chaos. "He arrived with me."

"Oh. Well." Lady Castlebury sniffed and brushed at a loose strand of her fading red hair. "At least there is that."

"In fact, Damon and the duke are decent friends now, Mother. He came with me to offer support to both Nora and Rainville."

"Given his penchant for discovering secrets, how did your husband not uncover this one before it was too late?" Lady Castlebury stopped pacing and sent her displeasure careening toward her oldest daughter. "It would have been helpful to us all."

Carenza tipped her head to the side, and a blonde curl fluttered around her neck. "Are you blaming Damon for not predicting their kiss?" She shook her head and smiled gently with the question. "That is not what he does, Mother. No one could have predicted that Nora would kiss the duke. I'd wager not even Nora knew it would occur."

"I didn't!" Nora burst out defensively. "I never in a million years would have kissed Rainville of my own accord."

"Then why did you?" The question came quietly, steadily, from the center of Nora's giant bed. Leave it to Lottie.

"Because I wasn't thinking!" Nora rapped her knuckles against her head. "I was not thinking at all."

"Now that lack of thought has led us here to this scandal, young lady." Nora's mother glared across the bedchamber at her. "And if the duke refuses to do what is right and proper, then we are all ruined."

"He'll do what is right," Carenza reiterated. "Rainville is an entitled, spoiled duke, yes. But he is one with a conscience." She held out a hand, and Nora went to it and wrapped it in hers, thankful for the comfort. Her sister leaned close and whispered for her ears only, "Do not forget it was he who helped when the Revivalists attacked the Meadowlark Tavern while I was there."

"What say you, Carenza?" their mother demanded to know, narrowing her blue eyes on them. "You know how I feel about whispered conversations!"

Nora squeezed her oldest sister's hand in reassurance and placed her head on Carenza's shoulder, calling out, "We know, Mama. She was merely mentioning the duke's very fine carriage, that is all."

"Thank you," Carenza uttered softly into Nora's hair.

"Why yes, it is indeed a fine carriage. I daresay the Somerton family crest is so beautifully executed in style on the door."

"Given the current circumstances, Mother, I do believe you will have the opportunity to ride in his fine carriage quite soon," Lottie said cheerfully. "It does one tremendous good to look on the bright side of a situation, does it not?"

"I hate this," Nora whispered to Carenza, her head still tucked on her sister's shoulder. "I hate *him*."

"Rainville or our father?" her sister whispered back, her apparent confusion making Nora snort softly with wry humor.

"Both," she admitted, and sighed heartily.

"We all have strong feelings about Father from time to time." Carenza patted her arm comfortingly.

"That's the real reason Catamount isn't here, you know." Nora raised her head briefly, noting her mother in animated conversation with Lottie, and lowered it again to continue in a low tone, "He refuses to be around Father."

"I know." Carenza sighed. "I know." And she fell silent, gently rubbing Nora's arm.

"I have to do this, don't I?" Nora whispered in resignation. It wasn't a choice. It had never been a choice, not from the moment their lips touched, and others had borne witness to it. "I *have* to marry the duke."

Chapter Six

"Do try to appear as if you like me, minx." Rainville kissed the knuckles of her gloved hand, to all the world looking the doting fiancé as they danced together at the Fentons' annual ball the following night.

Nora was not fooled. "I *don't* like you." Bouncing lightly from the ball of one foot to the other in rhythm to the music, she asked, "Why should I pretend otherwise?"

They each raised a hand and pressed palms together before repeating on the other side with the opposite hands. With every brush of his hand against hers, breath hitched in her chest—and by the time Nora spun away from Rainville she was breathless and jittery, with a vague sort of excitement shimmering within her. For what, she knew not. Only that it had bloomed the moment she finished her spin and came back to him. Grew acute.

She met his molten amber gaze and promptly lost her count, stepping on his toes through his dress boot. "So sorry," she mumbled, her cheeks flaming. It wasn't her fault she'd tripped! Rainville had been blessed with physical perfection. When he focused those unusual dark gold eyes on her, rimmed with thick sable lashes, she forgot how to think. Infuriating truth, that.

"Pretending affection toward me, your *fiancé*," Rainville said, "provides less fodder for the gossip hounds."

They touched palms, spun away. Nora gulped stuffy drawing

room air into her lungs and tried to slow her racing heart, her skittering pulse. Composing her expression, she was ready when they came together once more. "Let them stare—I care not." It was true, mostly. "I'll not pretend to want something I do not."

Another spin, another coming back together. "We both know that's a lie." He smirked. The words trailed hot and taunting down the side of her neck, and Nora shivered. "We both know what you truly want."

Brazening it out, she threw back her shoulders inside her favorite blush-pink gown and met his penetrating gaze with her own, bold and unafraid. "You are a competent dance partner. I will give you that."

Unholy amusement lit the depths of his lionlike eyes. "Is that what you're calling it in your head to appease your innocent sensibilities?" As they drew close again, moving in time to the uplifting dance rhythm, he leaned down, smelling intoxicatingly of sandalwood and man, and said in scandalous confession, "I prefer to call it fu—"

Nora tripped, breaking stride, and nearly fell. Rainville's large, strong hand steady on her elbow kept her upright. Unnerved by his touch and crude language—they caused a restless, itchy, fiery feeling to flare inside her—she yanked her arm free and snapped, *"Your Grace."*

"My lady," he shot back. "Quite the temper you possess."

"I don't have a temper," she said, suddenly quite parched and hot under the chandeliers with so many dancing bodies pressed close. "My father has the temper."

"Ah, a family trait, then."

If the blasted man smiled at her with such a smug, mocking expression upon his beautiful countenance one more time, she was going to scream. Or punch him. Or both. And not a single person in the world would blame her for it. "You are not endearing yourself to me." That was the truth. To compare her with her father was an egregious sin, to say the least.

The only thing stopping Nora from stomping on his foot and making a scene was the uncomfortable fact that such behavior would humiliate her family—and with her impulsive kiss to Rainville they were already on tenuous ground, though her parents were endeavoring to make it appear to all Society as if it had been a kiss between an already affianced, in-love couple. And she knew a woman could do nothing in this world that did not reflect well or ill on her parents and siblings that did not reflect on the family name. Not upon her as an individual, but upon her *entire* family. That she could wield such power and yet be so incredibly powerless at the same time cramped Nora's brain and made it hurt.

A woman must be perfection. Always.

Not act perfect. Not appear perfect. She must *be* perfect. Or else shame befell her entire house and name.

It was for those sorts of reasons that Nora exposed the worst male oppressors with her paintings. Made them experience a moment of frozen fear and humiliation, loss of control. Perhaps it would foster change for the better, compassion—for arrogance lived and bred in ignorance. Her eternal hope was to be a creator of change. Women deserved better.

"What has you staring so intently?"

"Hmm?" Nora blinked and drew her attention back to Rainville. "I'm sorry, Your Grace, did you say something?"

Something flashed in his gaze, lit the golden depths like a torch, and he drew close with the dance. "You should call me Joss."

A shiver ran down her arm, and she glared at him. "That would imply an intimacy between us."

His intense gaze dropped to her mouth, and his nostrils flared. "You're right, it would."

"So, why would I do that?" Her heart skipped a beat at the way his voice dropped low and went gravelly.

"Because we're about to become *very* intimate, minx." And suddenly he was smiling, a wide, wicked smile that whisked her breath right out of her chest.

"Never!" she whispered fiercely, her stomach quivering in anticipation, betraying her. With a stubborn hitch of her chin, Nora pushed off Rainville's hand with hers and began to spin away, nerves and anger jostling for residence in her chest. As she twirled, she caught sight of one of the Castlebury footmen near the drawing room doors waving to her beside the potted palms, and it sent alarm ringing through her. *I forgot,* she mouthed silently to him, her eyes wide and apologetic as she suddenly remembered the plan for the last finished painting she had meant to reveal tonight. That had never happened before! Goodness, how had she forgotten so easily?

Because of him.

Instantly alert, Rainville narrowed his eyes suspiciously on her. "What are you about?" he demanded, his wide shoulders going tense beneath his dark dress jacket. *"Nora."* Her name dripped warning, and she inwardly flinched.

"I... I misremembered something." Nora raised a gloved hand behind Rainville's back as he drew close, and she tried to wave off the footman. The timing of everything felt all wrong. "It is nothing of consequence."

Lie.

"Please tell me that I was the last of your targets, that there are no more paintings." His sharp words rang in her ears as the dance came to an end and polite applause made its rounds.

Nora swallowed indelicately around the lump in her throat. Her heart thumped hard and fast behind her ribs. How had she forgotten this painting, this plan already set in motion? "I can promise nothing," she said with an upward twitch of her chin, and felt his hand clench into a fist at the base of her spine as he escorted her from the drawing room dance floor.

"Why?" he growled down at her. "Blast it, *why?*"

"Because some men deserve it!" Nora whispered fiercely, fighting a surge of near panic, and tried to wave off her footman once again.

"Besides, I was not going to be here tonight. It's only due to you and our awful situation that I am even present. I was set to be at home curled up in bed with a favorite novel before you went and ruined everything by kissing me."

"Oh, so it's acceptable to humiliate another nobleman if you're not present to witness his downfall. Is that it?" The anger in Rainville's tone had her spine snapping straight with defensiveness. "Am I to take it, then, that you wished to witness *my* demise?"

"Of course I did," Nora snarled, quite suddenly feeling trapped and overwhelmed and perhaps a tiny bit remorseful. Unable to communicate across the drawing room effectively with the footman, she gave up and lowered her hand to her side.

"Congratulations, then," Rainville drawled in a decidedly frigid tone. "My demise is your platform for greater social status and success. Well done, my lady. Well done." The current of anger running under his words sent spears of unease shooting through Nora's belly.

"I never wanted you," Nora shot back under her breath. "I meant it when I said I despise you! You're every bit the same as the others I've painted."

"And yet you are stuck with me, and I with you."

"It could be a marriage in name only. We need never see each other again after the wedding." Yes, that could be quite acceptable to her. "Why, I think that could be a splendid idea, actually."

"You think you can keep your hands off me?" The way he said it with such a note of mockery sent Nora straight to fuming. "Here, let us test." With that, Rainville clasped her hand, placed it firmly in the crook of his arm, and led her from the dance floor directly toward the drawing room exit.

"What do you think you're doing?" Nora asked the duke, and tugged at her hand to no avail. The blasted man held it firmly in his. "People are watching!"

They weren't that she could see, not any more than they had all evening, but still. They were in public, after all.

"Let them watch." His free hand came up to cover hers as she wrapped it around his crooked elbow. How doting and endearing it appeared—when in truth Nora found herself unable to disengage from his grasp. Oh, the infuriating man!

"I could shout, you know."

Rainville scoffed and cut her a glance. "I think not. You've too much loyalty to your family to see them ruined over some juvenile temper tantrum."

"*Oooh*, I really, *really* dislike you!" To the point of loathing. There, she admitted it. She loathed him with all her being.

"You won't be the first bride to detest her husband," the horrible man drawled, effortlessly leading her toward the double doors that led out into the much quieter hall.

"I hear congratulations are in order, Your Grace."

Nora felt the flex of muscle under her palm, sensed the tenseness that gripped Rainville's body. "Lady Lingbottom," he said, briefly inclining his head.

"And congratulations to you." The elegant woman turned dark eyes on Nora, assessed her slowly from head to toe in a way that made quite clear her unspoken disapproval. "Let us get a good look at the lady who captured the Duke of Somerton, shall we?"

※

Joss silently cursed and tugged Nora close to his side. He didn't trust Lady Lingbottom for a moment. "Rainville. The Duke of Somerton was my father," he bit out.

"And also you," the countess replied lightly, her attention directed at Nora. "What a coup for you, my dear, to catch a *duke*."

Nora stiffened under his hand. "Considering my father is one of the most powerful and connected men in England, I rather doubt there are any concerns on the matter of who of us is truly the *catch* here," Nora replied coolly, impressing him. It appeared that not only did his future wife have a backbone, but also that she did not shy from confrontation with him or anyone. A rare and refreshing trait, that.

"Ah yes, the Earl of Castlebury. Such a strong alliance this engagement brings between two most distinguished houses. We are all very intrigued to know how it came about, for it seems so sudden!" the countess exclaimed, and snatched a flute of champagne from a passing servant in crisply ironed livery before downing the contents in one extended gulp.

"I assure you," Joss replied easily when she was finished, "that it was anything but sudden."

"Oh!" Lady Lingbottom said, seemingly taken aback, but her dark eyes turned hard and her knuckles white as she gripped the stem of the crystal glassware. The smile she pasted on her beautiful face appeared innocent and sweet, however. "Well, I am so delighted for you both."

Her excellent performance did not fool Joss for a moment. "Good evening, Lady Lingbottom." Cradling Nora's glove-covered hand in the crook of his elbow, he led her away from the unpredictable countess before she could lash out and strike like a poisonous viper.

"You, sirrah, are incorrigible," Nora whispered angrily as he led her toward the drawing room exit and tried to pull her hand from his grip. "She is clearly one of your women."

"My women?" Joss replied, lips twitching in amusement as he held her steady to him. "Pray tell, how many *women* do you believe I have?"

"I don't have to dignify that question with an answer," his little minx retorted with a sniff haughty enough to make Winston proud.

"Jealous?" Joss watched her while he voiced the question, noting the flush of color that rushed over her cheeks. "You *are* jealous," he teased, a part of him secretly pleased. Another part wondered just exactly what it meant that he was pleased about it—and feared the answer.

"I am not!" Nora snapped, and succeeded in yanking her hand from his grip.

He gave her a pitying look, enjoying her response immensely. "It's nothing to be ashamed of, sweeting. It's an affliction that ails us all upon occasion."

"I am *not* jealous!" she hissed, shooting daggers at him with her magnificent green eyes. "I do *not* like you, and I did *not* enjoy our kiss!" Suddenly she looked sharply around, spotted the exit nearby, and hastened them through. "Here, I will prove it."

Heat unfurled and warmed his blood as he realized he would let Nora *prove it* to him anywhere, anytime she wanted. In private or in front of a bloody audience at Rhodes, he cared not, so long as her mouth was on him.

And that was blasted telling, wasn't it? Shot a hole right through the story he had been telling himself about how much a fluke their kiss had been. That it had been a strange, random flare of attraction.

Wrong.

"Here we are," Nora stated with grim resolution, and pulled him behind a heavy brocade curtain to a tiny alcove that housed a rather tall, ugly vase and was barely wide enough for his broad shoulders. "Now you'll see how I really feel about your kisses." With a yank of his starched cravat, she pulled him to her and planted her lips squarely on his.

Desire sparked wild inside Joss. Groaning softly, he leaned into the kiss, his senses immediately reeling at the feel of her lush, plump lips against his. *Vixen,* he thought, and thrust his fingers into the silky hair at the nape of her neck, loosening several strands from their pins to tumble down onto his hands. "More," he demanded, and molded his lips to hers, stroked her tongue boldly with his. Teasing. Taunting. *Daring* her to take more of him.

Nora sagged against him, her incredible curves flush against the ridged planes of his body. "See," she panted after dragging her lips from his, her beautiful eyes fluttering open, dazed, and unfocused with passion. "Your kisses do absolutely nothing for me." She looked at his mouth and slowly licked her lips, as if trying to capture every last taste of him. That she seemed unaware of her actions made it even more powerful. Such innocent seduction. It sent lust straight to Joss's loins and turned him to stone.

"*Liar,*" he whispered affectionately, stroking his hands boldly up the front of her gown to cover her breasts. "My kisses make you wet."

She gasped but did not deny it.

What he wouldn't give to hike her skirts and slip his finger between her slick folds, to taste her, to fill his tongue with her glorious dew—to discover her desire for himself.

A bellow rose from the drawing room suddenly, cutting through the passionate haze surrounding Joss. He jerked to his full height and turned his head, his attention racing toward the sounds coming from the drawing room, all excited, scandalized whispers, and exclamations. "*Nora,*" he growled, just knowing it was her fault.

"Who did this? This is an outrage! That is not me! I do not look so foolish! How *dare* anyone besmirch me. I want this person found now! Oh, they will pay for this! They will *pay!*"

"Lord Lambert, please calm down," Lord Fenton pleaded over the murmuring crowd. "Get that painting out of here now!" he commanded, undoubtedly directing the order to a nearby servant.

A snicker, a rush of hushed voices, as members of the *ton* erupted at the new scandal.

"*I will have heads for this!*" the marquess roared, and something in his tone had the hairs on the back of Joss's neck rising.

"Damn you," he swore, catching the satisfied gleam in Nora's eyes before she could mask it. He latched on to her shoulders and bent, brought his gaze even with hers. "What in hell has Lambert done to you?"

Color rushed her cheeks and her shoulders trembled slightly under his hands, but still she tipped her chin defiantly, her peridot green eyes flashing. "It's what he does to his servants, rather. Especially the maids. He's... he's *vile*, Rainville."

Doors crashed open, bouncing off the walls and rattling several expensive vases on their custom pedestals. Through a slight crack in the curtain, a fuming Lord Lambert strode through into the hall, still ranting and making threats, rage crackling off his lithe frame. As he passed by, Joss had a moment of true unease when he realized that Nora could be in real trouble from retribution for her paintings. If not Lambert, then another. Any peer she'd targeted could seek vengeance.

In a flash he realized what he needed to do until the heat cooled down and people forgot about the scandalous paintings by Anonymous.

"Damn it," he swore again, tightening his grip on her shoulders. "*Damn it.*"

He had to get Nora out of London.

Chapter Seven

They were married two days later by special license at Tipton House with every Castlebury family member in attendance. To witness her humiliation, no doubt. All the men were currently ensconced downstairs in the study enjoying a pre-ceremony drink or cigar or some such male thing, even though it was barely eight in the morning. The women congregated in the drawing room.

"I told you it was quite unnecessary, Mother. Catamount and Crawford have better things to do with their time than stand by, watching me hand my life away to that big, golden fool." Nora tugged at the bodice of her cream wedding dress, express made by modiste extraordinaire Madame Toussaint, feeling uncomfortable and hot in the airy, lightweight fabric. "Is it hot in here?" She fanned her face and scrunched her pert, freckled nose as she glanced around the drawing room of her childhood home, noting all the open windows. "It's hot in here, isn't it?"

"It is not hot at all," Lottie replied from her perch on a blue settee near the windows, leather journal in lap and her usual ink blots on hand. "In fact, it's rather pleasant in here. I believe it may be your nerves."

"No, no, it's *hot*," Nora insisted, fanning her face as rapidly as her hand would flap; her heart beat nearly as fast. "And this corset—it is too tight. I can scarcely breathe." To punctuate her point, she inhaled and made a pitiful wheezing sound. "I need fresh air."

"Where do you think you're going?" called Lady Castlebury, immediately following Nora out of the drawing room, then stopping in the hall in a swirl of gold silk skirts, pointing back through the doorway. "You're to be wed in there."

"No, I can't." Outside, under the sky. No ceiling, nothing boxing her in. That was where she desperately needed to be.

"Ceranora, come back here this instant!" Her mother's voice rose with each word, ending in a brittle shriek.

But Nora was not listening. Her feet propelled her down the hall toward the back of Tipton House, past the study doors half ajar. As she passed, she spotted her brothers—Captain Catamount of the Bow Street Runners, with his shaggy brown-blond head and tired green eyes colored so like her own, and Crawford, the handsome and polished prodigal heir with his pale blue eyes and perfectly trimmed mahogany hair—and Rainville, looking impossibly handsome in his moss-green jacket, ivory waistcoat, and tan breeches that hugged his muscular thighs indecently and drew her gaze, unbidden, to them. Trailing her eyes slowly upward, Nora caught herself just as the buttons on the flap of his breeches came into focus. Sucking in a breath as her face flamed, she yanked her gaze from the front of his clothing and peeked at his expression to see if he had noticed. His hot, intense gaze and knowing smirk confirmed that he, indeed, had. He raised his glass to his lips and slowly sipped, watching her the whole time, until she was past the door and out of sight.

"*Blast,*" she said fervently, and hurried toward the verdant back gardens of Tipton House. It was too early for this! Too early in the day to ruin her life. Too early for everything to change.

Pressure built in her chest to an unbearable degree as Nora burst from Tipton House. Sunlight—oh, blessed sunlight—washed over her face and down her neck, warm and comforting, stilling her movements. Tears sprang to her eyes, sharp and stinging, as emotion swelled, rose inside her like a mighty tide. "I can't do this!" she burst out to the birds chirping nearby in the apple tree heavily laden with growing fruit. The birds' sudden, startled silence sent her tears tumbling, free-falling down her heated cheeks to drop in great plops on her bodice, quickly soaking into the delicate fabric.

How was it fair that she should be so harshly punished for something so small, so *simple*, as a kiss?

A lifetime married to the Duke of Somerton? Of him being in control, making choices, dictating. Exactly as her father did.

When was *she* ever going to be in control?

Nora sucked in air, wheezing, unable to catch her breath. Tightness spread throughout her chest, gripping harder and harder, like the turn of a vise. Her pulse tripped and skittered, went racing out of control. "I... I can't... breathe," she panted, her voice thin and wavering.

"It's scary, isn't it? Trusting a man with your life?"

Nora turned around at the sound of Carenza's steady voice, a bare hand pressed to her abdomen, and found her sister a few feet away near the cluster of yellow roses their mother so favored, looking beautiful and poised, as always, in her pale blue gown and sunlit curls. "Utterly terrifying," Nora confessed. She *needed* to confess to someone.

"Here, let me assist you with your breathing. Bend at the waist and place your hands on your knees. There you go," her sister encouraged her when Nora had complied, sucking great gulps of air. "Deep, steady inhalations."

"It... was just... a... *kiss*," Nora asserted between pants, her gaze focused on the flat gray stones of the garden pathway beneath her feet and the springy clumps of fragrant thyme growing between them and blooming a delicate pinkish-purple color. "My life... should not be over for it," she pronounced, and wheezed again. A fat, furry bee fluttered into her vision and landed on a velvety bloom. How she wished to be that bee and fly away!

"Perhaps," her sister proposed gently, "it is not actually over."

Carenza placed a reassuring hand on her back, rubbing small circles. "Perhaps it is simply changing."

"I despise change."

Carenza laughed, light and easy, the sound reassuring to Nora's frazzled nerves. "You sound like Lottie."

"She is wise beyond her years." The pressure in Nora's chest loosened, eased at the comfort her sister provided through her touch and calm presence.

"If Lottie knew you said that, she'd be incorrigible." Carenza chuckled, still patting Nora's back. They fell into silence for several moments, simply listening to the bright chatter of birds and the gentle buzz of industrious pollinators soaking in the morning sunshine. After several more moments, Carenza asked, "How are you doing down there?"

Nora replied, not really jesting, "I'm considering taking up beekeeping in a far-off land under an assumed identity."

"That's the spirit," her sister replied good-naturedly. "Before you do that, however, you've a duke to wed."

With one last steadying breath, Nora straightened, looked her sister square in the eye, and blurted, "I'm so scared and I don't want to!"

Warm, sturdy arms whipped out and wrapped Nora in a fierce hug as Carenza said against her hair, "It'll be fine, darling. Rainville is trustworthy, I promise. I've entrusted him with my secret, and he's done nothing but honor that. Not told a soul that I am the Meadowlark. It's going to work out just fine, you'll see."

Clinging tightly to her sister, Nora sniffled and asked the question that haunted her most, embarrassment flooding her tone and burning her cheeks. "What about... you know? The husband-and-wife portion that Mother refused to tell me about when I asked. What of that? Will it hurt? Will it fit? How does one go about positioning oneself for the act? *How* does it fit? Is it like dogs? Horses? I have *so many questions!*"

Nora ended on a soft wail, fluttering her arms around helplessly before they went limp against her sides.

"Oh!" Carenza exclaimed, and squeezed her tightly but briefly. "Well, I'm no expert on the matter, but I'm fairly confident in saying that yes, it will fit, and yes, it may be a bit uncomfortable at first—but that it will ease in short order if he performs his job correctly."

"But what if he *doesn't*?" Nora wailed, overwhelmed with so much emotion. "What if he's bad? Or worse, selfish? Brutish?" A pause, and then, "Dear God, what if he simply doesn't *care*?"

"Oh, I doubt that he will be bad at it, dearest! From what I've heard about his mating prowess, the truth is quite the opposite," Carenza reassured her.

Nora raised her head and pushed away from her sister, eyes swimming with unshed tears. "That is decidedly not reassuring, hearing of his prowess with the ladies."

"I only meant that he is known to ple—"

"Thank you!" Nora cut in. Something fierce and feisty was flaring in her chest at the thought of Rainville in bed with another woman. Was it... was it jealousy?

Goodness, no. It couldn't be.

She *refused* to let it be. Jealousy implied a certain level of caring that she did not possess. She did not care for Rainville at all.

"Excuse me, ladies," came his deep voice from several feet behind them, followed by the sound of his boot heels rapping against the patio stones as he made his way across the garden to them, all languid, powerful grace.

Of course. Of *bloody* course he would arrive during such an intimate and private conversation. One that involved him.

"Go away," Nora grumbled, her cheeks flushing hot with self-consciousness. How much had he overheard?

"I'm afraid I cannot oblige you," he replied amiably before turning his attention to her sister. "My lady, I wish a word in private with

Nora."

"You cannot simply *call* me Nora," she protested, though her traitorous stomach fluttered with excitement at the sound of her name on his lips. "I have not given you leave."

"I can. You are my intended—therefore, the familiar address is warranted." The way Rainville said it, almost as if he was explaining it to a child, stirred up her temper. Which, in all honesty, she much preferred to the spurts of raw vulnerability that erupted randomly inside her and left her winded and feeling exposed and scrambling for the safety and shelter of her bluster, longing for the armor of her temper.

"Such a high-han—" she started, leaning into the comfort of her anger.

"I'll see myself back into the house," Carenza cut in, and squeezed Nora's shoulder in encouragement, letting her know without words that she could handle this moment, this challenge. "It's a beautiful day we're blessed with. Do enjoy it, won't you?" With that, she retreated into Tipton House, leaving Nora all alone in the garden with Rainville.

"The last time we were alone in a garden together, we ended up engaged," he commented, his tone easy. But his golden eyes watched her closely, intently, as he moved a few steps down the paved garden path toward her. His thick, muscular thighs drew her attention as they flexed under his finely tailored breeches. "This time, it seems, we are to be married. Husband and wife."

In an instant, the temper inside her was snuffed out and Nora gasped as that raw vulnerability rose inside her without warning and swallowed her whole. Her *everything* shook from the force of it. Her face crumpled. As tears sprang to her eyes again, Nora spun away and hurried down the garden path, further into the dense foliage planted specifically for privacy. She'd made it around a giant pink hydrangea bush and out of sight of prying eyes inside Tipton House before Rainville caught up to her.

The moment his hand touched her bare elbow, and she felt his heat, experienced the surge of giddy sensation that ran up her arm, Nora whipped around to him, making her curls bounce around her face in the most aggravating fashion. She swatted at them, shoving them out of the way. "Mother insisted I wear my hair in this style for the wedding, and at this moment I sincerely wish to chop it all off."

"That would be a shame." Rainville raised his free hand and collected a few ringlets, letting them slide around his long fingers. "Your hair is rather magnificent."

Unprepared for the compliment, and therefore unarmored, Nora felt the blow of his sincerity right to her heart—the last place she ever wished for Rainville to be. But oh, how her heart swelled from the hit with a sweet kind of tenderness and pride, brushing against that raw vulnerability darting about inside her. Nora's mouth dropped open and she stared, simply gawked at this man she must share the rest of her life with, completely at a loss. What did she do? What did she *say*?

His eyes, so strange and beautiful with their mixture of amber and gold, gentled. "Has no one ever told you that before?"

Nora shook her head, quite suddenly transfixed by the way his lips moved when he spoke and the small white scar on his chin, out of place amongst all his gold and bronze coloring. His scent filled her nostrils, and she breathed him in, wanting more. Wanting to kiss that little, pale scar and learn the story behind it. Wanting to forget he was one of *them*—one of the entitled, overprivileged men she so despised. To forget that marrying him was a blind gamble of the most terrifying sort.

Good God, how would he treat her once she was his wife, his property? What did her future hold with him? Would he endeavor *at all* to make her happy? How could two people who despised each other make a good marriage?

Did she even *want* a good marriage?

Nora focused on the thin, small scar running diagonally across

Rainville's cleanly shaven chin and uttered, "I don't want to be married at all." That was the closest she could get to admitting her fear to him, and her stomach squeezed tight with nerves. "We don't even like each other."

"True," he replied. "On one level we decidedly dislike one another. A lot."

"Agreed. You're entitled and spoiled," Nora pointed out, leaning the tiniest bit closer to him, catching his scent and melting a little inside.

"You're imprudent and infuriatingly willful," Rainville replied, his voice low and laced with a slow-burning heat—the kind that hinted at much stronger feelings concealed beneath the calm surface.

"Snobbish."

"Disrespectful."

Nora snorted, surprised by his candor. "Guilty," she agreed. "It seems you know me rather well, Your Grace." She absorbed the shock of that and blurted, "Tell me something personal about you." Something to tether herself to, something she could hold on to that reminded her, in the rocky days and years ahead, that he was, underneath it all, a flesh-and-blood man. That he was simply a person. Not a duke, or a peer, or a male with elevated status in Society—or even her husband. Something that anchored her to the truth that he was simply a human being, like her. Someone of equal footing.

Reaching over her shoulder, Rainville snapped a cluster of hydrangea blooms from the giant bush and went about tucking them behind her ear with a surprising amount of tenderness and competency. An unexpected combination, that, and it made her stomach flutter. "Something personal about me?" he asked, quirking an aristocratic brow.

Swallowing, her throat suddenly parched, Nora nodded. "Yes."

For several intimate heartbeats he assessed her, his eyes so warm and gentle—a stark contrast to every other time he had gazed at her in the past—that she felt suddenly stripped of all privacy, naked and exposed clear to her soul. "Never mind," she rushed to say, hoping to sever the tentative connection hovering between them.

As if he had not heard her, Rainville tipped his perfectly sculpted lips up at the one corner in a completely unexpected, unbearably adorable, boyish grin. "My fully christened name is the fairly terrible Joslin Bonaventure Rainville."

Nora's eyebrows shot to her hairline. "Your middle name is *Bonaventure*?"

"Ridiculous shite, isn't it?" He kept right on grinning, his eyes still gentle and glowing, his demeanor disarming and confusing her. Where was the brute who had tossed her over his shoulder without thought or care?

"May I call you Bonny?" She nearly smiled back.

"Only if I may call you Norabell."

Blast. "My father's slip?" she inquired, knowing it had to be. When he nodded in confirmation, she added, "Tell me something else. Something I'll not learn in another twenty minutes, when we..." She trailed off with a vague wave toward the house, unable to say the words. "You know. Something that will make this whole thing feel less terrible."

"I could remind you that it was your painting that brought us to this point to begin with, and that it is you who should be comforting me... but I shall refrain."

"How gallant of you," Nora drawled sarcastically, and raised a hand to touch the blooms he had placed in her hair. It was a nice gesture, that.

"I am rather gallant, it's true. Good of you to notice." The humor lighting his eyes drew her in like bees to flowers.

"Humble, too," Nora remarked, feeling the tenseness in her shoulders ease some at his banter. "*So* very humble."

"Nobody likes a braggart." Rainville smirked down at her, once again gently playing with the curls around her face.

"Precisely."

"I like your hair."

"You do?"

Rainville nodded. "It reminds me of sunrise in the West Indies, when the air is clear after a night of heavy rain and you can see for miles."

Her breath caught in her chest. Her hair? Sunrise? "Y—" She broke off and tried again as her heart began thumping heavy in her chest. "You have been to the West Indies?"

"Last year, actually. Hottest, most beautiful place I've ever seen."

"Well, I..." Nora trailed off again, so unused to compliments and flattery that she knew not what to say. Temper was her language.

He tugged her curl, bringing her gaze to his. "I think about you, even when I shouldn't."

The words, so softly confessed, sent her emotions tumbling. Blinking against the sting of tears, Nora gaped up at the man she was to call her husband. "But, Your Grace, you despise me."

"Ceranora, where are you?" called her mother from the patio of Tipton House. "It is time! Come inside now."

"Wait, I've one more," Rainville said quickly as her mother noisily made her way through the garden toward them, calling out every few steps. He gently gripped her curl, held her close.

Nora wasn't sure how many more of his confessions she could handle. "Yes?"

His gaze went molten gold. "I really want you to call me Joss."

CHAPTER EIGHT

AFTER SIXTEEN HOURS of intensely paced travel down well-worn pike roads, they arrived at Joss's favorite place on all the earth: his country home, Somerfield Park. Simply being there, even at two in the morning, as he was now, filled him with an ease he had rarely felt elsewhere in all his travels. A sense of rightness and purpose. This was his land, where his ancestors once bred and raised majestic thoroughbreds. Where he now raised his own special breed of horses. And where his sister drew comfort and healing after their parents' passing.

Somerfield Park was home, with its original tower and great hall and quirky additions. A place where he could let his guard down and be simply Joss. Not Rainville the duke, or the theatre owner, or the showman with the lush, expensive attire. But merely Joss. The man who loved to wake up early to catch the sunrise from the bare back of his favorite horse, who took great joy from his small Clydesdale breeding program. Who loved theatre because he possessed an enormous, tender heart and imagination rarely seen in a person past the age of childhood. But, just as his appetite was forever by his side, so too was his imagination, ever seeking matter, substance, on which to build a story.

Nora—she captured his imagination. And he knew—he utterly *knew*, and it terrified him—that if he looked beyond her surface, she would be the greatest story he would ever uncover. Better for them both if he left her alone.

Problem was, he didn't want to. Well, *he* wanted to—but his body didn't.

"Here we are," he said to Nora upon entering the bedchamber adjacent to his—in the west wing of the sprawling old manor house that had been built in the 1300s from nearby golden-colored Ham Hill stone. "This is to be your suite as the duchess of the estate. I believe Anna will attend you until your lady's maid arrives on the morrow from London. It was kind of you to give her the extra time to bid farewell to her family and friends." With a gesture around the spacious, well-appointed, peach-toned room, he added, "There is a separate sitting room through the double doors over there, as well as a walk-in wardrobe. My mother dearly loved her dresses and had the room specially designed when I was but a lad. I remember playing in there, getting lost among the colorful fabrics, and realizing at a young age that her dresses were merely costumes, a representation of the person in that moment she chose to be, that she chose to present to the world. It fascinated me." He recalled the memories now, and a smile streaked over his face, open and full of fondness.

"And now you own a theatre filled to brimming with costumes, and you wear rather sumptuous, finely tailored jackets of outrageous hues. I believe I may be beginning to understand you, Duke." His new bride glanced about the room, her arms wrapped snug around her, tired and beautiful in her rumpled wedding dress.

"Joss," he gently corrected her.

"Someday, perhaps."

"Mm," he grunted noncommittally, not really understanding his need to hear his name on her lips but aching for it all the same. Still, he refrained from pushing her further on it. Instead, he strode across the thick cream, peach, and gold rug to an oak door and grasped the hand-painted knob. "If you need anything, my chamber adjoins yours through this door."

Her eyes—oh, those eyes of hers, those liquid green pools of fire and defiance—rounded and filled with a mixture of curiosity and wariness. "Y-your chambers? Do you mean where you sleep? In bedclothes?"

"No," Joss replied honestly, biting the inside of his lip to keep from laughing out loud at the expression of sheer relief that rushed across her beautiful face as she stepped through the threshold into his most personal space. "I rarely sleep in bedclothes," he added just to taunt her. "Or any clothing at all."

She stopped so quickly that he almost plowed over her. Sidestepping, Joss slipped around her, noticing not for the first time how the top of her head barely reached his chin. Nora was big energy in a short, curvy package. "Do you... Are you implying... that you sleep in the... in the..." She trailed off and waved a hand about her, looking tired and overwhelmed and so very, incredibly beautiful. Wholesome and vibrant and innocently sensual.

Having her in his bedchamber at Somerfield Park—the one place that he had never, *ever* bedded a woman—did strange things to him. Somerfield was his refuge, his singular place to be at peace in the world and to express his truest self. To withdraw and renew. That Nora was now and forevermore a part of the landscape there sent him stumbling ill-equipped through a dozen emotions.

She thought she knew him?

Nora didn't know him at all.

But she desired him. He knew that from her painting. "I'm saying I sleep in the nude." Let his gorgeous, temperamental bride sit with that information. She, who was bold enough to paint him working himself, with her as audience. Sliding her a glance, Joss caught her just as she pried her eyes from the front of his breeches and her cheeks flushed an alluring shade of pink.

It was becoming increasingly clear to him that the audacious painter and the woman were not the same. Painter Nora worked from fire and fantasy behind the curtain of anonymity. Flesh-and-blood

Nora was far more innocent and skittish than she pretended to be.

In truth, she was much like a blustery, nervous filly.

And Joss knew exactly how to handle those. Never from the side. Always from the front, allowing them time to get used to his presence. "Take a look around, if you like," he offered, hoping to disarm her and help her relax. "Also, if you've a wish to redecorate Somerfield once you settle in, please let me know. I'm happy to accommodate. I only ask that you refrain from touching this room." It was exactly as he liked it.

"I confess, it's not what I expected. Somerfield *or* your bedchamber." Nora held her arms fast to her, but her natural curiosity had her strolling across the ancient hardwood floors, stopping to peek at the built-in shelves full of books near the fireplace. Before their arrival, his staff had lit the candle sconces around their bedchambers, and the flickering light played now over the elegant slope of Nora's neck and shoulders, beckoning him to her.

With effort he remained where he was and began to ease his jacket from his broad shoulders, feeling the day's hard travel in the knotted muscles of his neck. Once the jacket was removed, he draped it across the back of a nearby chair, his attention locked on Nora. His wife. A hot burst of primal possessiveness erupted in his chest at that truth, at the knowledge that she was his—this temperamental, aggravating woman who still had not shown an ounce of remorse or apologized for nearly ruining him with her painting.

What did he make of it all? Make of *her*?

"I expected your chamber to be more similarly decorated to your theatre," Nora remarked as she trailed a finger along the glossy surface of his small writing desk where he kept his journals and sketches. "This is rather a contrast to the opulence of Rhodes."

A contrast. A contradiction. Like him.

And like everything he felt about his new bride.

"Does this room displease you?" he asked, surprised at his own caring. Joss shifted his weight onto his other leg and surveyed his private chamber with fresh eyes, as Nora now did, taking in the unusual and unfashionable color palette of soft buckskin and stone-gray tones, the simple lines of the furniture, the large, earth-toned rug—and his favorites: several lush potted palm plants and framed paintings of horses. But no gold embellishments, no silk or satin—only simple, peaceful comfort.

If she disliked his most private space, it felt like a personal rejection. A judgment of who and what he was. A silly notion, he realized, but the fact remained that he wanted Nora to like his bedchamber. And he refused to examine why that was. As he often told Winston, denial was his preferred state of being in the world. Changing that now would be out of character for him.

As if summoned, his valet knocked on the door and poked his head inside, pushing his glasses back up the bridge of his nose with a chubby index finger. "Pardon me, Your Grace, but I wished to inquire about any culinary needs you might possess after your travels."

"It is rather late," Joss noted quietly. His gaze strayed back to his new wife and caught upon the graceful curve of her bare neck, flickering pale gold in the candlelight as she continued perusing his most recently acquired books. They remained in his chambers until he finished with them and sent them to join the rest in his library, located in the manor's original round tower.

"It *is* late, Your Grace. You are correct. Yet your loyal staff know of your particular food consumption needs and wish to offer you a platter of select meats, cheeses, and breads baked just today in anticipation of your arrival."

At the mere words, Joss's stomach clenched in hunger and gave a mighty growl, alarming his bride and sending her head whipping in his direction. "Beg pardon," he said with some chagrin to her. "An unflattering consequence of my size, I'm afraid."

She quirked a brow, inquiring over her shoulder, "Possessing a rumbling stomach?"

"Possessing the appetite of a plow horse," he deadpanned, enjoying the way her responding laughter lightened her eyes and sent them twinkling.

"It costs more to sustain him in feed than a bull at the height of its health and virility," Winston shared loudly. "We've resigned ourselves to his ways, alas. We understand he is not actually trying to behave like a child with his constant asking for snacks, even if that is often the result."

"I am not to be blamed for my hunger pains, or the need to satiate them." Joss's gaze drifted back to Nora when he said the words, and a whole different type of hunger began to gnaw at him.

"Perhaps His Grace would enjoy the prepared platter being brought up, then?" Winston inquired with a smugness that signaled he well knew Joss would like a platter of food. "Should you wish anything, Your Other Grace?" he added, his attention fully on the new duchess.

"Does our duchess wish a platter as well?" called Gomery, his age-roughened voice unmistakable, from the hallway.

"How long has he been standing out there?" Joss hooked a thumb over his shoulder toward the door.

"Several minutes, Your Grace," Winston replied, pushing his glasses once more into place. "He arrived upstairs with me. We wished to see to the comfort of you and our lovely new duchess."

"Aw, you missed me," Joss jested, enjoying the flush creeping up Winston's round cheeks.

"Thank you, Winston," Nora spoke up from across the bedchamber. "But I've no need for a platter to be brought up."

"Excellent, Your Grace. Your Other Grace." Winston inclined his head at Joss, a small, satisfied smile fleeting across his lips. "I shall return momentarily with sustenance." His head briefly disappeared from the doorway before returning. "Congratulations to you both. We are so pleased that you are here, Duchess Somerton. So very pleased."

"Indeed we are, Your Grace!" called Gomery from the hallway.

Nora lightly laughed, curving her lips in the most beguiling way—and Joss had the fiercest urge to see them curved, all beguiling, around *him*. Right around his...

"Sausage!" Gomery hollered in his raspy old voice, and the sound echoed down the hallway. "There is also sliced sausage on the platter, Your Grace! Are you certain your new bride should not like some sausage? It is quite plump and juicy."

"No thank you," Nora replied with a shake of her head. "Sausage fills me up."

"Is that not a good thing, Your Grace?" the butler inquired from the hall, his confused voice carrying through the opening in the door that Winston occupied. "Good sausage should always fill a lady up."

"I would rather not be stuffed full of sausage at this late hour of night," Nora protested kindly. "I generally prefer to have my sausage in the morning. But I do thank you for the offer. Another time, perhaps?"

Joss was dying.

Absolutely *dying*.

"I say, Your Grace, are you well? Your countenance has turned an alarming shade of red!" Winston declared, his brown eyes dancing with mirth behind his wire-rimmed spectacles. He knew *exactly* what had Joss so choked up—and was enjoying his discomfort immensely.

"Is His Grace unwell?" called out an alarmed Gomery. "Make way, make way!" The elderly butler appeared in the doorway and pushed his way right past a protesting Winston.

"Ouch, watch your elbows, you old bugger!"

"Your Grace, I'm coming!" the butler declared, ignoring the huffing valet.

"Gomery, I'm quite fine," Joss said around a bubble of laughter, waving his worried servant away. Offering his bride an apologetic look, he explained, "We stand on very little formality around here."

"I can see that," she replied.

"Your face is quite red, Your Grace. Are you well? It is your appetite, isn't it?" The butler whipped his hand out and pressed the paper-thin back against Joss's forehead. "I detect no fever." With a satisfied nod, Gomery concluded, "You're famished, is all. I'll see to your sausages myself."

"It's an *entire* platter of edibles, for crying out loud," Winston muttered. "All sausage and only sausage would be a bit much."

Joss coughed, covering his laughter. But then he made the mistake of glancing at Nora once more, noted the slight shaking of her shoulders, and realized she was withholding laughter as well. "I'm fine," he assured his butler gently, knowing how much Gomery cared. In some ways—several, in fact—the old man had been more like a father to him than his own. Gomery had always made time for him, doing tasks suited for the nanny or the governess, simply to inquire about what Joss thought on this subject or the next. It was Gomery who had first noticed his love of theatre. Not his mother or father or the nanny. But Gomery, the whip-thin butler from Derbyshire. "You needn't trouble yourself further."

"You are never any trouble, Your Grace," Gomery clucked, and Joss let him fuss for a few more moments.

Laughter, warm and light and disbelieving, came from near the bookcase.

Joss speared Nora with a glance and arched an inquiring brow. "You disagree with Gomery?"

"I most decidedly disagree. You, sirrah, are nothing *but* trouble."

"Smart lady has your number," Winston chirped, dimples appearing in his rounded cheeks. "You will do well here, Duchess Somerton."

"Thank you." Nora inclined her head, blushing slightly—and it was the most becoming one Joss had ever seen.

"Oh! Her Grace has not yet toured the grounds of Somerfield

Park," Gomery stated with a brush of his hand down his still-crisp livery. "On the morrow, if you like, we shall see to remedying that. I'm quite certain Lady Claire is looking forward to seeing you again, as well."

"And I her," his bride said, sounding genuine. "It has been several years since I have had the pleasure of her company."

"Her temperament is best suited to the quiet life of the country. It will be good for her to have some fresh company, however. I know she is fond of you and your sisters," Joss said.

"Then I look forward to visiting with her tomorrow," Nora replied, stifling a yawn.

"Good heavens, the food!" Gomery suddenly exclaimed, and jolted into motion. "Winston, assist me."

Joss's valet released a long-suffering sigh and swept a hand across his ample belly toward the bedchamber door. "After you, old man."

"I'm not old," Gomery countered, shuffling on arthritic knees toward the exit.

"You're older than dirt."

"And you're rude."

"I make no claims to be otherwise."

"All right, you two. Take that bickering downstairs." Joss shook his head and crossed his arms over his chest. "It has been a very long, very full day."

"Quite right, quite right." Winston reached out and escorted the elderly butler toward the door. "We will get right on that platter of a *variety* of meats and cheeses. Someone will be up with it momentarily."

"Welcome to Somerfield!" Gomery called out as he shuffled out the door. "We are delighted you are here, Duchess Somerton."

"We truly are." Winston nodded his agreement and pushed his glasses back into place. "Tomorrow, we shall show you all of Somerfield. For now, we bid you a good evening."

And with that, Joss's servants ushered themselves noisily from the room, leaving him alone with his bride on their wedding night.

Their *wedding night*.

Heat flared in his stomach, but one look at Nora standing alone by his bookshelves, looking exhausted and overwhelmed in her travel-rumpled dress, had him realizing it was not to be one of *those* wedding nights. "Should you like to retire for the evening?" he asked her softly, tipping his head in the direction of their connecting door.

He could read the emotions rushing across her face. "I—"

"It's all right," he reassured her before walking over and placing a chaste kiss on her cheek. "There will be plenty of time for that."

"I—"

Tenderness washed through him. "Sleep tonight, Nora." He took her by the hand and led her to the adjoining door. "Perhaps you'll dream of me."

He, without doubt, would be dreaming of her.

"I, um... Well, are you certain, Your Grace?" She worried her bottom lip, casting him a glance through her lashes. The sheer sexuality of his bride, so wrapped in innocence, tumbled right through him and lit him on fire. "I *am* rather peaked."

"Of course," he instantly murmured, wanting only her comfort and sense of safety—even if his ballocks ached with need for her. "Call me Joss." *Please.*

How he needed to hear his name on her lips as she begged for him, shattered apart in his arms.

"Mm," she evaded, and shrugged a shoulder.

"Another time, perhaps," he suggested, his tone gentle. Inside, however, he felt increasingly *ungentle*. Desire pushed at him, licked its flames along his flesh. Ignited him.

"Perhaps," she softly agreed as her gaze dropped, her thick fan of lashes shielding her eyes from him. Yet he saw the flash of undisguised interest when she landed upon the front of his breeches and saw the bulge there. Saw the way her mouth opened slightly, like an invitation.

Joss bit the inside of his cheek to keep from groaning. *Hard.*

"Well," she raked her gaze back up to his and cleared her throat, color high in her cheeks. "Good night. I shall see you on the morrow."

"Yes," Joss quietly agreed, and laced his fingers together behind his back to stop himself from reaching for her.

Christ, how he wanted to touch her.

"Nora," he whispered as she hesitated at the door.

"Good night!" she squeaked weakly as she fled through the doorway.

The moment the door slammed shut between them, Joss dropped his forehead to the glossy oak that separated him from his wife and released a growl of so much pent-up lust that he shook from the force of it. "Fuck, Nora," he groaned as he steadied himself with one arm near his head, and lowered the other to his straining erection, needing her, needing release. *"Fuck,"* he breathed, fumbling with the opening of his breeches and taking himself in hand.

Suddenly he was there, in Nora's painting, working his cock as he imagined her hungry, greedy eyes watching him, wanting him. Stroking moisture from his tip down his stony shaft, pretending it was her mouth on him, warm and wet.

"Nora," he panted, nearing release. His hips jerked with each feverish, desperate stroke.

Want me. Damn it, Nora. Want me back.

The orgasm started in his ballocks and tore through him at blazing speed, dimming his vision and making him lightheaded. Joss gasped and slammed his fist against the door, rattling it next to his forehead, the sound a thundering boom in the quiet bedchamber.

"Is everything well over there?" Nora called from the adjoining room, concern etching her tone.

"All is fine," he rasped. "Go to sleep, Nora."

"I—"

"Sleep," he growled.

"But I heard—"

"*Nora.*"

"No need to be rude, Rainville. I was merely inquiring."

"Do you truly wish to know what occurred?" His voice went warm and intimate. If the lady really wanted the truth… "Because I will tell you."

"Good night!" his wife chirped, and then all fell silent. Not even a bedpost creaked. The only sound at all was the fire in the hearth breathing.

That's what he thought.

Chapter Nine

Winston and Gomery made good on their word, and Nora spent the whole of the next morning and early afternoon touring the house and grounds of Somerfield Park. An extended engagement it was—in part due to the massive size of the estate, and partly due to the creak in poor Gomery's knees and Winston's predilection for frequent stopping to catch his breath. Bless their hearts for insisting on personally escorting her.

"Thank you so much for this thorough and informative tour of Somerfield. It has been most educational." Such an abundance of history the estate contained! For three splendid hours she had been immersed in its story. "It's wonderful that the original tower and great hall are still a part of the manor."

"Not merely a part of it, Your Grace, but the *heart* of it," Winston said as they leisurely made their way through the extraordinary gardens that extended behind the manor and down the slightest slope toward the massive barn made of the same warm-colored stone as the manor. A veritable meadow of flowers spilled, tumbling wild across the lush English countryside—trees of various sizes and shapes appearing here and there, providing shade and a feast for the eyes. And all of it was Rainville's. *Hers*.

Incredible.

"I confess that I've not been much for the country before now." Her father had made the quiet and isolation less than ideal. London provided ways to avoid him. "But *this*," she gushed, spreading her arms wide to soak up the sun. "This is perfection."

"Lady Claire takes great care with the garden," the butler replied, pride obvious in his voice. "She has quite the touch with living things of all types."

"I daresay she does indeed," Nora agreed, amazed at the lush, sprawling grounds surrounding her. "Have you any knowledge of her whereabouts? I should like to compliment her skill in person."

"Most likely she is with the horses," Winston predicted as he squinted against the bright summer sunshine. Raising a hand to offer his eyes shade, the valet pointed with his other hand toward the barn. "You'll find them in the large stone barn down the hill on the right. The smaller barn off to the left is for the other livestock."

"Ah yes, because Somerfield was once a highly regarded thoroughbred farm. I remember," she added with a pleased smile. "Such regal creatures deserve a dwelling all their own."

"That is the Somerfield way," Gomery boasted.

"Oh, I believe I just caught sight of Lady Claire entering the nearest stall from the paddock," Winston said, pointing a little further to the right.

"She'll be grooming that pony of hers now," the butler agreed. "Wonder what knitted contraption she's come up with today for her Cuddles to wear."

"I do not know about you, but I was quite keen on the pony leg warmers she knitted that slid over the hooves and up the pastern. They appeared most functional *and* fashionable," Winston mused. "Even Mrs. Whipple approved." He turned his brown gaze to Nora. "Our housekeeper disapproves of nearly everything."

"You asked Lady Claire to knit you a pair to go over your own winter stockings, didn't you?" Gomery drawled, and cut the valet such a look that Nora snorted in sheer, surprised amusement.

"You know I did," Winston professed proudly, his chest puffing, "and you are simply envious."

"Lady Claire is an avid knitter?" Nora inquired, feeling her own twinge of envy. She couldn't knit for the life of her. Paint? That she could do with flourish and skill. Any sort of needlework only left her with bruised and punctured fingers.

"A truly talented one, at that." The old butler beamed.

"Well. Thank you so much for your time, gentlemen. I believe I shall make my way to the horse barn and seek out the company of Lady Claire." Perhaps she might then learn where Rainville had disappeared to directly after breaking his fast that morning, for she had not caught sight of him since. It felt decidedly like he was avoiding her.

Shouldn't *she* be the one doing the avoiding?

Truthfully, she did not know what to do about anything at all anymore. Her life had turned upside down. Nothing was the same as it was two weeks ago. Right down to her own name. "If you please, I shall take my leave and wander to the barn."

"Would you like an escort, Your Grace?" Gomery offered a thin, sharp-angled elbow.

"That is kind of you to offer, but I shall be fine on my own." A few minutes of solitude to sort her thoughts and feelings would be most welcome.

"As you wish, Your Grace."

"Thank you," she said around a smile, and began the stroll to the barn, admiring the building and the way the sunlight seemed to make it glow, as if lit from within. It truly was beautiful, and she could picture it as it had been, full and bustling with elegant thoroughbreds. The second-floor hayloft must have been a favorite place for many of Somerfield's young residents throughout the year. Undoubtedly, the sprawling view over the rambling hills from up there was remarkable.

Suddenly quite curious to see it for herself, Nora picked up the skirts of her simple sprigged muslin day dress and began to run across the manicured grounds, laughing in delight at the sense of lightness and joy it brought. It was hard to be miserable, even given the circumstances, on a day such as this one. The sunlight poured warm and glorious over her, the air brushed her cheeks with a softness not found in London Town, and the heady scent of ripening hayfields and summer flowers filled her nose in the most satisfying way.

Perhaps... perhaps she could be happy there.

After romping through the gardens, Nora soon came to the edge and slowed to a walk, appreciating immensely the tidiness of the estate, how the grass remained trimmed right up to the stone fence and double gate that demarcated the area between the manor house and the working portions of the estate. A line of lovely lilac bushes with their deep green leaves paralleled the wall and continued down the gently sloping hill, leading away to the open patchwork fields below. Taking a moment to stop and appreciate the refreshing air and expansive view with so many dazzling, verdant shades, Nora tucked a few stray pins back into her hair and marveled at the peaceful scene before her. Somerfield Park truly was something.

What did it mean that such a place belonged to Rainville? That his home felt so welcoming and calm. Had she... had she possibly misread him? Misunderstood him?

And why on earth did she feel slightly relieved at the notion that she *had*?

A commotion came from the other side of the double gate, catching Nora's attention. Mindful of potential free-roaming livestock, she crept up to the gate and peered through the thick wooden slats. "Oh my," she breathed in surprise when she spotted what had caused the ruckus. Rainville, bare-chested and sweaty, stood in the clearing between the massive barn and the gate as he bathed a giant horse. Or rather, he tried to bathe a horse. The horse had other ideas.

Biting her lip to keep her laughter inside, Nora bent her knees and lowered until she had a perfectly clear view of Rainville between the gate slats. Placing her hands on the gate for stability and curling her fingers into the smooth wood, she leaned forward for the best possible view and forgot all about her quest to find Lady Claire. Nothing short of a stampede could stop her from ogling her half-naked duke.

"Goodness," she whispered as she pressed her forehead against the gate rail, all awareness coming to focus on a single point: Joslin Bonaventure Rainville. Her husband.

He was *magnificent.*

Bronze and gold and glistening in the sun, his body appeared strong and tough in a way that was so very different from her softer feminine form. With each move he made, his muscles flexed and bunched, all sinew and power and grace. Without his tunic on, Nora noted just exactly how broad his shoulders truly were, how lean his corded waist. She discovered, and instantly became transfixed by, the golden hair lightly dusting his chest and running in a line down his stomach, past his belly button, and disappearing into the low-slung waistband of his trousers. For several heartbeats she watched the trail of gold, until a restless, needy feeling swelled inside her and she tore her gaze away.

"Deuce it, you aggravating equine. We can do this the hard way if you'd rather, but we are doing this. You've rolled in a something so foul-smelling my eyes tear up when I am within three feet of you. I don't know what in blazes possessed you to do it, but you bloody well need a bloody, bloomin' bath." Rainville's voice dripped frustration. "You're not a damned dog, rolling about in fresh piles of shite. Now, be still, Cinnamon Sticks. This is serious." He stepped toward his huge bay horse with a bucket of water and immediately stopped and turned his face away. "Christ, horse, was it something *dead?*"

The draft horse nickered and bobbed his huge head.

"No, not dead?" her new husband replied, and pushed the heel of a hand into one of his eyes then rubbed. "Rotten, then, perhaps?"

This time the horse stretched its neck and reached out to nudge Rainville in his side with its muzzle, rocking him and spilling water from the bucket in a great slosh to the ground. The stallion nickered again, almost as if it was saying that yes, he had rolled in something rotten. The communication and bond between the two were plain to see. As was the gentleness in Rainville's touch when he reached out and petted the Clydesdale.

"Who are you?" Nora whispered as she absorbed the sight before her. The duke that she knew from London was resoundingly different than the duke she watched now. London Rainville dressed differently, behaved differently, was arrogant and dismissive. London Rainville had deserved her painting, her scorn for the way he had treated her. But this Rainville, this man who had treated her so tenderly and with consideration since walking into the garden of Tipton House the morning of their nuptials—he perhaps had *not* deserved it.

Who was the real Duke of Somerton? And why was she suddenly experiencing a niggling, sinking sensation in her gut, like she had done something wrong?

"You are in a particular mood today, horse," Rainville grumbled with a shake of his tawny head. Damp tendrils curled at the base of his neck as he went about bathing his mount, though he surely had stable hands aplenty for the task. Again, Nora felt that immediate, fierce urge to bury her fingers in his luxurious waves. Were they as silky to the touch as they appeared? Gripping the gate slats even tighter, she shifted her position for greater comfort and continued to stare unashamed at her husband's extraordinary physique. Men did it, so why shouldn't she? Especially when the physique was so… so… virile.

And it was *hers*.

Heat streaked unexpectedly through her belly, bloomed between her thighs, and her heart made a great big thump. Nora gasped.

Oh God, Rainville was *hers*.

This man she had detested, this spoiled duke—this man she suddenly did not remotely understand—was hers for now and the rest of her days.

A whimper tumbled from her lips, a small, overwhelmed sound. Nothing more, only a tiny noise, but Rainville heard it. His dark blond mane whipped up and around, and the muscles in this abdomen tightened, rippling with the movement as he stilled in his task and listened.

Squinting against the sunlight, he scanned the area and called out as he tossed the cleaning cloth into the water bucket, "Who's there?"

Nobody. Why, there was no one there at all! Certainly not Nora staring obsessively at Rainville's incredible body like the versions of her in her painting of him. She instantly recalled the scene she had created, and the placement of Rainville's hand on the canvas. Her gaze shot to the front buttons of his trousers and the impressive bulge there, and she whimpered again, feeling quite… needy. Hungry. It was a sharp, startling sensation.

"Nora, is that you?" Rainville tipped his head to one side, standing tall and regal in the clearing near the stone barn, his hair and trousers damp from bathing his horse. "I know the sounds you make." He smirked and raised a hand to the flat expanse of his abdomen, then began to lazily scratch at an itch there. The motion drew her gaze right back to the front of his trousers.

Knowing she was good and caught, Nora rose from behind the wooden rails, smoothed the front skirts of her dress, and tipped her chin high against the embarrassment before entering through the gate. "Why, Rainville, I had no idea you preferred to bathe with the animals," she said tartly, not knowing what else to say, as her equilibrium was decidedly off-kilter at the sight of all his manly muscles flexing and showing off.

"They are oftentimes preferable to people," her duke replied, still narrowing those watchful eyes on her as she walked across the flat, hard-packed dirt toward him. "Take this beast, for example." Rainville reached out a sculpted arm and patted his horse's neck, and Nora lost all train of thought at the way his shoulder muscles bunched and rolled, such an obvious display of his masculinity. "He's a smelly bugger when he gets into something, but a more loyal friend I've never had."

Cinnamon Sticks lowered his massive head and nudged Rainville in the back with his muzzle.

"I think he agrees," Nora replied. The closer she stepped to Rainville, she noticed, the faster the butterflies fluttered in her stomach, until they were in constant motion when she was directly in front of him. Raising her gaze to his, she wasn't sure what she would find. But she certainly did not expect to discover him staring down at her with warmth and something akin to restrained passion in his beautiful eyes.

He raised a tanned hand and cupped her cheek, gentle as water. "How did you sleep last eve?" he asked quietly. He began to caress her skin lightly, slowly.

"Quite comfortably," she answered truthfully, her mind quickly emptying of all rational thought with each brush of his thumb over her skin. "You?"

"Abysmally," he murmured, dropping his gaze to her mouth. "Absolutely terribly."

"That's a shame," Nora whispered, her breathing going shallow with building anticipation. Would he kiss her again? Did she want him to?

Yes.

Good God, yes, she wanted his kiss again. This man she no longer despised, but who confused her more than ever. Who lit a fire in her body like nothing she'd experienced before. Who lit a fire in *her*.

"It's your fault I slept not a wink." Rainville's deep, cultured voice washed over her, hot and surprisingly intimate, and turned her knees to liquid. "I should make you suffer for that, the way that *I* suffered."

"How did you suffer?" she breathed, brushing her breasts lightly against his bare chest as she leaned into his hard, athletic form.

"With *want*," he whispered against her lips with searing intensity.

"I suffered with *so much want* for you."

Nora gasped, and heat flooded her body. "What—" She broke off and swallowed. Her throat was instantly parched bone dry. "What did you do?"

Something in Rainville seemed to snap at the question. His eyes went hot and filled with a dangerous, sinful glow. "I came for you," he growled. "I came so goddamn hard for you, minx."

Molten liquid pooled between her legs, and Nora moaned, innocent to why her body responded to his words in such a way yet pressing fully against him anyway. "I don't understand what that means," she confessed a little desperately, her eyes wide on his. Her breasts ached for his hands to cover them, to mold and shape them as he pleased. His tone of voice... The way he said it... A flush swept up her cheeks. Heavens!

"I know," he grunted, splaying his hands over her curved hips, and yanked her flush to him. "Damn it, I know. And it's going to be my undoing."

"I—"

He stopped her with a kiss. *Thank God,* something inside her sighed, heady with relief. Nora melted into him and gave in to the urge, tangling her fingers in his thick, tousled mane. *Finally.* At last, she knew what it felt like. A part of her never wanted to let go. Holding it, holding *him*, felt so right. With only him as an anchor, she gave herself over to the kiss, sweeping her tongue against his boldly.

He growled and flexed his hands over her hips. Then his fingers curled and dug into her flesh, held her tight. "Damn you," he swore darkly, pressing his straining manhood against her. *"Damn* you."

Helpless to do anything but cling to Rainville as passion swept through her, Nora kissed him with utter abandon, chasing his tongue with her own. When he lifted her off the balls of her feet, holding her to him, she merely moaned her agreement. A tingling, floating sensation spread throughout her body.

"Oh! I see that I have arrived at an inopportune time," came an amused female voice from somewhere in the distance, cutting through the haze of desire fogging Nora's brain. "I shall return later."

Rainville groaned softly in protest but gentled his hands on Nora and lowered her to the ground. "Claire," he said in greeting, his voice huskier, rougher than normal as he stepped away and turned to his Clydesdale resting nearby in the sunshine. "What excellent timing."

"Lady Claire," Nora rushed to say as she smoothed her skirts and turned her attention to her new sister-in-law. Her body protested the loss of Rainville's big, strong frame against her. "It is so good to see you again."

"Is it?" his younger sister replied on a laugh. "For it appears to me that I had horrible timing."

"Oh, that you had," Rainville grumbled with his bare, tanned back to them, and began leading Cinnamon Sticks into the barn. "That you most definitely had."

"Well, that's lovely, then, isn't it?" Lady Claire beamed and held out an elbow toward Nora in invitation. "I am off to the village, and since I've already ruined the moment between you two, I would be thrilled to have your company."

"Of course, I'm happy to go," Nora immediately replied, taking the offered elbow. It would give her time to sort out her complicated feelings.

"Perfect. It shall allow me time to divulge every embarrassing memory I possess of my brother for your great amusement."

A shadow suddenly fell across her vision as Rainville appeared at her side, golden eyes glowing in annoyance. "I'm coming along."

Chapter Ten

An hour later, Joss continued to curse his sister and her terrible timing, even after the three of them had set off for the village. Unspent desire agitated his body, made the movements stiff and unnatural. Nora appeared frustratingly unbothered, however.

"I confess, I do so enjoy a good ramble." His sister pointed across a field to the black-and-white cattle grazing idly. "There's always something of great beauty to appreciate, if one but looks."

"I suppose those cows are beautiful, yes," Nora agreed amiably, scrunching her pert nose in an adorably thoughtful manner. "Their contentment is quite admirable."

"I challenge you to name a person in possession of such fully embraced satisfaction."

"My sister believes we silly humans have much to learn from our animal brethren." Joss kicked at a clump of dirt along the well-trod lane and turned his attention to the cows under discussion. Several grazed along the hillside, swatting their tails every so often at a fly or some other annoyance. "I cannot say that I disagree with her."

"Is that so?" Nora's gorgeous green eyes widened in disbelief. "I would think the Duke of Somerton above learning anything from anyone, much less from a docile bovine."

"Not so at all!" Claire declared, startling the cow closest to them. It raised its head and stopped chewing, flickering its ear in their direction. "Joss is the most ardent proponent of listening to the wisdom of the natural world, especially our dear animal friends."

"I confess it did appear that he and his horse were having quite a discussion when I chanced upon them earlier."

Joss grunted, knowing his bride had "chanced" upon him for several minutes before he addressed her. It did funny things to him inside, knowing she had watched him. Clasping his hands behind his back, he strolled along the lane to the village, enjoying the play of light dappling through the leafy green trees overhead. "Cinnamon Sticks has many opinions, most of them revolving around his feed. He gets cranky if I don't hear him out."

"My brother is deflecting and being modest." Claire shoved him playfully in the shoulder, her hazel eyes full of sisterly consternation. "A kinder, more sensitive person I've never met when it comes to living creatures, big or small."

"It's humans I'm rubbish with," Joss teased, knowing it wasn't entirely true, and winked down at Nora. Her instant blush charmed him far more than he wanted it to and warmed his chest right around his heart. He coughed, startled by the sensation.

"Are you well?" Nora immediately asked, concern etching her pretty face.

"I am," he reassured her, though he was not entirely certain. Far too much occupied his thoughts, and most of it related to his bride.

Both women looked at him with great skepticism.

"I am!" he insisted, rather uncomfortable under the close scrutiny. Changing the topic, Joss cleared his throat and said, "There are several shops in the village you might enjoy perusing with my sister, but I thought it worth mentioning the art supply shop at the east end of the village square. It surprises with such a large variety, given its small size. If you've a need for any supplies, it will be sure to have what you seek."

"Oh, new paints!" Nora's mesmerizing eyes lit up, liquid green pools of delight. "That would be most excellent indeed. I did not pack any of mine, given the haste with which everything commenced."

"Imagine my shock when word reached Somerfield of your wedding!" Claire exclaimed happily, a bright smile upon her face. "Joss married was the last news I expected to receive."

"Yes, well, we simply could not wait." Joss flicked his bride a glance, catching the flush of pink covering her cheeks. "Could we, Nora?"

She met his gaze, and the power of the connection caught him off guard. "No, we could not."

Stumbling, Joss swore and righted himself. "Blasted tree root."

"Pray, do not get me wrong," Claire said in all earnestness to Nora, clasping her lace-gloved hands tightly in front of her as they strolled along the picturesque lane. "I am desperately pleased for your union." Stopping suddenly, his sister reached out and took Nora's hands in hers. "When I was informed that he had chosen you for his bride, I nearly wept with gratitude. You and your siblings were always so kind and welcoming to me at social functions. Though I struggled greatly with the crowds and conversations and loud noises, you treated me with warmth and not at all like the social failure that I truly was. I am so very pleased to have you for my sister." With that, she threw her slender arms around his bride, rustling her plain muslin dress with the movement, and hugged her quite tightly.

Love, fierce and devoted, coursed through Joss for his sister as he watched her hold close his wife. That Nora embraced her back with equal feeling had his throat constricting and going tight, had the backs of his eyes stinging. It was… Well, it was a beautiful thing, seeing his sister happy. It had been so very long. So very long indeed.

"I believe it is I who am the grateful one," Nora declared, and resumed walking with Claire's arm linked with hers. Joss trailed behind, watching the two of them with tenderness in his heart. "A sister with knitting talents such as yours is a prize indeed. Winston promised to show me the ankle warmers you recently made him when

I returned to the manor."

"Pish posh, I don't know that my creations are so grand," Claire demurred, but the smile that flitted across her face told him how much Nora's compliment truly pleased her.

"They are ingenious!" Nora countered cheerfully. "Why, when I heard of the sweaters you knitted for your pony, Cuddles, I confess that, at first, I was confused how it fit on. But then dear Gomery informed me that you split the sweater down the middle and created a row of buttons from which to secure it back together once positioned correctly, and I was so very impressed! Such creativity and ingenuity, dearest. Truly."

"I am in the process of knitting a matching set for Joss and his Cinnamon Sticks." Claire leaned close to his bride and whispered loudly, "I hope to finish before Christmastide. It is rather a lot of yarn, you know. Both of them are so very large."

Nora threw back her copper-blonde head in delighted laughter, exposing the graceful column of her throat above the bodice of her pretty dress, and Joss had the strongest urge to bury his nose there and breathe her in until he was saturated with her scent, knew it by heart. "I heard that," he grumbled.

"Your size is not exactly a secret, brother." The sassiness in Claire's tone made him smile. So very excellent it was. Try as he had after their parents' deaths, he was not their mother. It was exceedingly obvious now how desperate for female companionship she had been.

Perhaps... perhaps his marriage to Nora was not a completely awful thing after all.

For several minutes Joss pondered that possibility while his bride and his sister chatted happily ahead of him, the swish of their skirts a rhythmic, repeating sound amongst the varied birdsong. Bright bursts of sunshine swathed them in warmth, before returning to the coolness of the shade provided by the massive trees lining the road. Sweet, fragrant summer grass swayed in the gentle breeze, growing tall as his knees against the rambling stone wall paralleling the lane. Taking it all in, Joss let the peace settle over him and lull him into a lovely state of calm.

Ah, Somerfield. Every single time.

His home, his refuge, his retreat.

Nora's now, too.

Pressure in his chest broke him out of his reverie, and Joss turned his attention to his wife, felt the pressure increase. Before he could wonder at it, a sound came from the distance. Joss glanced over his shoulder and saw the slender cloud of dust that signaled an approaching rider. "Ladies," he called in warning. "Rider incoming." He had not realized how close they had come to the village. It was just up ahead around the bend in the road now. Riders and carriages were to be expected near the bustling little market town, but apparently his head had been in the clouds.

Stepping to the side of the road, into the grass, Joss raked a hand through his thick hair and slid Nora a glance. She was deep in conversation with his sister about some sewing or knitting technique, and he took the opportunity to study her. The way the sunlight shimmered in her hair, pulling out bits of gold and red in a dazzling display. Her coloring, so perfectly fair and peach-toned, and the slight smattering of freckles across the bridge of her nose. The gentle slope of her shoulders. She was wholesomeness and grace and subtle fire in an intoxicating, infuriating mix.

Or, at least, she *had* been infuriating. Now Joss wasn't entirely certain what she was.

"Ahoy there!"

Ripping his gaze from the delightful scenery of his wife's bosom, Joss glanced up at the sound of the rider approaching, noting with some surprise a gentleman he recognized. "Lord Lambert."

"Good day to you, Your Grace." The marquess looked down at the three of them from his mount. "Ladies."

"I am rather surprised to see you here, this far west of London." Joss inclined his head in greeting, noting the very fine horse upon which Lambert sat. "Excellent bloodlines in that one. It's plain to see." Powerful lines, deep chest, long, graceful legs.

"Why, thank you, Your Grace." The marquess smiled at them, though his dark eyes somehow lacked the lightness such an action usually provoked. "That is a fine compliment, indeed, coming from one who so excels in horsemanship and breed stock."

"Is this one your doing?" Joss inquired, and held a hand outward, palm down, for Lambert's horse to sniff in greeting. "It bears a striking resemblance to your mare that I watched win at the Downs."

"I am honored you remember, Your Grace." The marquess beamed, and his glossy bay mount shifted restlessly from hoof to hoof in a sort of prance of restless energy. "In fact, this is a full brother to that mare."

"Exquisite creature." Joss squinted against the sun and inquired, "What brings you to Somerton from London? Am I correct that your country estate resides near Bath?" Perhaps the lord had found a place nearby to let.

"You are indeed correct that my estate is near Bath. But it is you, Your Grace, that brings me out this way."

"Me?" Joss arched a brow. He and the marquess had never been more than polite acquaintances. Fencing partners at the club on occasion, but nothing more. It was most curious.

"In fact, I am just coming from Somerfield Park. Your footman informed me of your jaunt into town, and I hoped I might catch you," Lambert explained. "I am glad I was able."

Out of the corner of his eye, Joss noticed his bride inching away from the marquess, her jaw set in a tense line. He recalled her words about the marquess and how he treated his servants. Was that why she scooted away now? Or was it her guilty conscience over her painting? Either way, she appeared quite miserable. And for some godforsaken reason, he abhorred the notion of her misery, this woman who had been bent on his ruination.

"Pleased as I am to see you out here in the wilds of the country, I am afraid I've quite given my promise to these wonderful ladies and shall have to promenade on into the village to fulfill my duty. I am ever at their mercy," he added, sliding Nora a glance.

She met his gaze and blushed.

"Of course, of course. I completely understand, Your Grace." Lord Lambert reined in his antsy and spirited mount. "It is a business proposition I wish to put to you, and clearly this is an inopportune time. Shall I be so bold as to request an audience at your earliest convenience, Your Grace?"

"You shall." Joss nodded agreeably. "I've a full schedule until the end of the week. Return to Somerfield then and we shall discuss what is on your mind."

"Excellent, Your Grace." The marquess preened and shifted his weight in his saddle. A subtle movement, yet his mount immediately responded, backing up several steps and turning to face down the road toward the village. "I've an inkling you will be quite pleased with what I propose." He tipped his hat down at them, his dark eyes unreadable. "Good afternoon, ladies. Your Grace." With that, he motioned his mount into a canter, taking off at an easy pace down the lane.

Joss watched him go, curious about the marquess's proposition. Clearly Nora's painting had not scandalized him past the point of pariahdom. Or if it had, the marquess enjoyed a particularly close relationship with King William's niece. Such an alliance could weather all manner of storms.

It could also provide a beneficial connection for Joss and his theatre. To have such a patron as Princess Victoria… or even the king himself! He would have no need to fear a financial desert ever again. Or his theatre's position amongst the most elite performance stages in London.

"I'm so blasted glad that *gentleman* is gone," Nora grumbled with a scowl, lifting her skirts and setting off again at a fast clip down the road toward the village. "Now, let's see about new paints, shall we?"

Joss noted her dislike of the marquess and followed at a leisurely pace.

His new wife was an interesting one indeed.

Chapter Eleven

The brisk air of Somerton carried the distinct scents of fresh bread, blooming flowers, and the occasional whiff of horse manure. Joss walked with his new wife and sister, enjoying the beautiful day… and perhaps the view of his beautiful new bride with her coppery curls and lush figure swaying alluringly beneath the fabric of her dress. Her citrine eyes sparkled with curiosity as they approached the quaint little art store nestled between a bustling milliner and a fragrant bakery.

"How do you find Somerton's market?" he inquired, a slight smirk playing on his lips, knowing by her delighted expression that she approved.

Her gaze wandered over the vibrant market stalls. "I must say, it's quite charming."

Before them stood Crimson Canvas, the art store renowned throughout Somerset for its array of high-quality paints, brushes, and canvases. The wood sign above the door was a painted carving of a brush dipped in rich red paint.

Pushing the door open, Joss ushered them all inside. The interior was a treasure trove for any artist. Wooden shelves lined the walls, displaying an assortment of colorful oil paints in every shade imaginable. The scent of linseed oil and fresh canvas permeated the air. It was creativity and inspiration personified.

"Welcome to Crimson Canvas, Your Grace!" a sprightly man with graying hair greeted Joss, bowing slightly. "I am Mr. Bennett, the new proprietor. How may I assist you today?"

Joss nodded in acknowledgment. "Mr. Bennett, this is Her Grace, Duchess Somerton. She has a penchant for painting, mostly oils, and I thought it fitting to introduce her to the best art store in all Somerset."

Nora's eyes widened with delight as she took in the shop's offerings. "It's magnificent," she whispered, awe in her voice.

His sister wandered off to inspect a display of fine brushes, leaving Joss with Nora and Mr. Bennett.

"Allow me to show you our finest selection of oil paints, Duchess Somerton," Mr. Bennett said eagerly, leading Nora toward a series of meticulously organized shelves. "We have hues imported from Italy, vibrant pigments from France, and, of course, our local Somerset oils."

Joss watched as Nora's eyes darted from one paint tube to another, her fingers gently caressing the colorful labels. "What do you think?" he asked, his voice laced with genuine interest as his gaze lingered on her elegant fingers.

She hesitated for a moment before selecting a few tubes of cerulean blue, burnt sienna, and emerald green. "These will do nicely," she said, a soft smile gracing her lips.

Joss turned to Mr. Bennett and instructed him to prepare a selection of brushes, canvases, and other necessary supplies for his wife. "Make certain to include only the finest quality," he added, meeting Nora's gaze. "It is for my duchess, after all." Warmth bloomed in his chest at the words. *His duchess.*

"Thank you, Rainville," Nora grumbled, her voice ripe with consternation, nearly making him laugh. "You've been incredibly generous."

He met her gaze, momentarily lost in the depths of her gorgeous eyes. "It's my pleasure," he replied softly, realizing that it truly was. Seeing her happy *pleased* him.

What the deuce was he to make of that?

"Thank you kindly, Mr. Bennett. Your store is quite something." Nora said, moving toward the exit. "Have a lovely day."

"You as well, Your Grace!" Mr. Bennett called after them.

As they stepped out of the Crimson Canvas, Claire rejoined them, her arms laden with an assortment of sketching pencils and charcoal sticks. Her normally reserved demeanor seemed to soften slightly, replaced by a tentative curiosity.

"It appears we've all found something to our liking," Joss remarked, eyeing his sister's newfound treasures.

She laughed, a faint pink tinting her cheeks. "I thought I might try my hand at sketching," Claire admitted shyly. "Perhaps capture some of Somerton's beauty on paper."

He turned his attention to see Nora smiling warmly, looking thrilled with the idea. "That sounds delightful! We could spend our afternoons painting and sketching together. I could teach you some techniques, if you'd like."

"I would like that very much," Claire confessed.

"Shall we explore the rest of the market?" Joss suggested, eager to distract himself from the emotions swirling within him.

Nora nodded. "Lead the way, Your Grace."

"Joss."

"No."

"Someday."

"Mm."

"Am I missing something?" Claire asked, the bridge of her nose wrinkled in confusion.

"Nothing," Joss murmured, though it was very much something. It would be a sweet, satisfying day when Nora said his name.

As they set off for their leisurely stroll through the market square, a fleeting image of a familiar silhouette caught Joss's eye, sending a sudden jolt of surprise coursing through him. At the edge of the bustling crowd had briefly stood a woman whose elegant posture and striking dark hair were unmistakable. *Seraphina*.

What the bloody blazes was she doing there?

Had she really been there? The moment had been so fleeting. He glanced around, scanned every corner. Yet there was nothing.

Joss's heart pounded as he struggled to comprehend her potential presence in Somerton, a world away from the glittering ballrooms and scandalous soirées of London. If she was indeed there, what could possibly bring Lady Lingbottom to this quaint Somerset town, far removed from her usual haunts and admirers?

What reason other than *him*, that was.

Joss shook off the unsettling thought of Lady Lingbottom, attributing the silhouette to his imagination playing tricks on him. With a discreet exhale, he redirected his focus, determined to immerse himself in the present moment as they strolled along.

However, his deuced thoughts continued to drift, haunted by the imagined specter of Seraphina, until his sister leaned forward, her eyes bright with a mischievous glint he had never seen before as she confided in Nora. "You know, I've been thinking," she began excitedly. "I have a rather... shall we say, unconventional aspiration?"

Nora's ruddy eyebrows arched in curiosity, and her gaze flitted between Claire and him. "Do tell," she urged, intrigue lighting her green gaze.

Claire took a deep breath, her cheeks flushed with color. "I've been knitting these charming little items of clothing for our pets, as you know," she blurted, a hint of pride evident in her voice. "You know Winston loves his leg warmers. And it occurred to me—wouldn't the peerage simply adore the idea of dressing their beloved dogs and fine horses in such fashionable attire?"

Joss coughed and tripped over his own damned feet. What had she said? Peerage pets in knitwear?

Nora's lips twitched with a playful smile, and her eyes danced with amusement. "Pet clothes, you say?" she mused, her voice laced with intrigue. "That does sound rather... avant-garde."

Claire nodded eagerly, seizing upon Nora's encouragement. "Imagine the possibilities! A cashmere button-front for Lord Pelham's prized poodle, or perhaps a tweed vest for Lady Wilmington's spirited stallion."

Joss cleared his throat, his gaze locking with Nora's as he joined in the spirited conversation with a chuckle. "You know, Claire, I daresay you're onto something," he admitted. Nobles loved all sorts of novelties. "I can just picture it—the latest fashion craze sweeping through London's elite, with duchesses and earls clamoring to outfit their pets in your bespoke creations."

"And who knows," Nora added, her beautiful eyes dancing, "perhaps we'll even see a few esteemed gentlemen sporting your designs at the next soirée."

Claire leaned in close to them both. "You know," she began, her gaze flitting between them, though she avoided looking Joss directly in the eye. "I may appear demure and reserved, but I assure you, there's more to me than one assumes."

Joss's eyebrows shot up at the boast. He was fascinated by the glimpse of his sister's hidden depths. When had this change occurred? Or rather, where had this version been? The last thing Claire had expressed to him was the need to distance from the pressures of London life. "Oh? Do tell," he encouraged her, happy and relieved for this turn of events.

A playful smile turned Claire's lips as she continued, eager and earnest, and tucked a strand of golden-brown hair behind her ear. "I've found myself yearning for a bit more adventure of late, a taste of the excitement that lies beyond Somerton," she said, her eyes twinkling with anticipation. "Not a lot, mind you. Only a little. If my pet sweaters were to garner attention in London Town, who is to say I wouldn't seize the opportunity to showcase my talents on a grander stage? There would be nothing wrong with that. Why, I might even spectate a boxing match while I'm there!"

Boxing match? His sister? Who was this sibling? "Claire has always surprised me," Joss said. Though it had been a long while. "She's not one to be underestimated."

Nora nodded. "Quite obviously. And what of this boxing match you mentioned?" she asked, clearly curious. "I recall Joss mentioning once his admiration for a boxer named Longfellow."

Claire's eyes sparkled with sudden and unexpected interest. "Ah, yes, Aaron Longfellow. I've heard rumors of his prowess in the ring. Should I find myself in London Town, I should very much like to experience the exhilaration of one of his boxing matches firsthand."

Not on Joss's life. "Oh, that's not happening," he warned.

"We'll see," his sister replied with a flippant shrug, then she linked her elbow with Nora's and continued walking.

Joss stopped dead and rocked back on the heels of his boots with a huff, looking from his sister to his new wife, completely flummoxed. Who the deuce were these women?

And why did he suddenly feel so decidedly outmatched?

Chapter Twelve

THE NEXT DAY, Rainville took her on a picnic.

"What prompted this special activity?" Nora inquired as they set out on horseback. Somerset's glory was on full display, with its summer greens and fields of wildflowers, blissful blue sky, and warm, fragrant breeze. Truly, it was a perfect English day.

"You packed your new paint kit, correct?" her husband responded, a smug, excited gleam in his eyes. He looked so beautiful to her, riding tall and strong upon his mount. Cinnamon Sticks pulled at the reins, impatient and eager to stretch out his legs. "Steady, my friend," Rainville murmured to his horse, and rested a hand against his neck, lightly stroking.

At the sight of her husband's long-fingered, tanned hands, a flush of heat swept up her spine. What would it be like to have those strong, capable hands on her? Would he be slow and steady, or demanding? Gentle? Would he take his time and caress her everywhere?

A small sigh escaped her lips, and Nora started, jerking a bit in her saddle. She cleared her throat and motioned to her horse with her free hand. "This mare is so very lovely; I feel as if I cannot accept her. It's too much."

Her husband cast her an unreadable glance. "I'm only sorry I could not do more for a wedding gift on such short notice." He came up alongside her as they rode over rolling green fields, so fit and masculine and beautiful it almost hurt to look at him. Nora's chest squeezed tight as butterflies took off, fluttering wildly in her stomach. "Fanny here is a gem of an equine. She knows every command, is stable as they come, and loyal as a dog. She'll follow you around the paddock without a lead rope of any kind."

"She's perfect," Nora replied with a stroke of her hand along the mare's shiny chestnut coat, deeply touched by Rainville's thoughtfulness. "Truly perfect."

"I wished you to have a reliable mount. One that I knew would never bolt or shy or give me any cause for concern or worry while you were on its back."

That was... Well, that was really rather kind of him.

"You're not at all like I expected you to be," Nora blurted, and instantly regretted it. Embarrassment washed through her.

"Is that so?" he replied in an easy, casual tone. "Pray tell, what did you expect?"

Blushing hotly, she turned her face away from him and inhaled a deep breath for steadiness. Ever since she had arrived at Somerfield Park, she had felt so off-kilter. About herself, about life, about *Rainville*. Nothing was what she had believed it to be. Especially not him. It had her questioning herself in ways that she never had before, had her feeling uncertain. Her, the woman everyone thought of as brazen and bold.

Sometimes she wondered if the brazenness wasn't simply armor she wore to protect the soft, sensitive soul underneath. It was odd that, since arriving at Somerfield, she had not flared with temper even once. If she was so inclined, she might believe it to be the fresh country air. Or the beautifully situated manor. Or the delightfully quirky servants who had so quickly captured her affections. Yes, perhaps it was all of those things that had kept her temper in check.

Or, perhaps, Rainville had something to do with it.

Never had a man treated her with such consideration and care. Which Nora knew to be an entirely odd thing to think, considering they were wedded and thoroughly stuck with one another for the rest of their lives, because her loathing of Rainville had set off the entire chain of events that led them here. Yet the fact remained that since he had appeared in the garden at Tipton House, he had behaved in such a decidedly different fashion than the arrogant, insufferable Duke of Somerton that she barely understood them to be the same person! And this duke tugged dangerously at her emotions, her *desires*. Even ones she hardly knew she possessed until he grabbed hold of one and paraded it in front of her face, forcing her to see herself and what she wanted from a new vantage point.

"I expected the same impertinent man who tossed me over his shoulder without a single thought given to me." That was the good and honest truth.

"It was not without thought, minx. Never without thought." He shook his tawny head at her. When he looked at her again, something flickered behind his gaze—a spark of heat. A flame. For what? *Her?*

Nora scoffed, all bluster and befuddlement. "Before that night at the Meadowlark Tavern, you had not given me a moment's notice." Oh, how she wished that were not true.

Wait. What on earth was she *saying*?

Nora's horse halted, exactly as if she had spoken the words aloud. "Carry on." She leaned over the large, gentle mare's mane and gave her a reassuring pat. "You're an excellent listener, dear."

"I am reassured to witness another conversing with their equine the same way I do." Rainville gave her a lopsided, boyish grin. "Crazed horse people."

Completely unarmed and unprepared, Nora felt the unfiltered power of his charm slam into her like a runaway four-in-hand. The wind whipped from her body, left her dizzy and breathless and shaky. She must have appeared ready to faint, for in the next moment Rainville was there, his horse pressed next to hers as he steadied her with both of his strong hands on her body. Hands with a roughness and strength not typically found in men of his social class.

"Easy there, minx. I've got you. Steady on." His deep voice, so calm and assured, comforted her and excited her at the same time. Verily, it turned her into knots inside, all tangled with want and desire and couldn'ts and shouldn'ts and *did he* or *didn't he*. The heat of him seared her through the fabric of her riding habit.

"Thank you," Nora attempted to say, but her words came out breathless.

"Is it the mare? Is she too tall? Are you feeling vertigo?" Questions burst one after the other from her duke's finely sculpted lips.

Touched at his obvious concern for her health, Nora smiled, though the corners of her lips ached with the effort. "She is perfect."

"Food, then." Rainville nodded, apparently having decided something of import. "You need sustenance."

"I'm certain you're quite right," she whispered, intrigued by her husband's behavior. "Shall we continue to our picnic destination?"

"Yes," he agreed, turning his beautiful, lionlike eyes on her. "I'm famished."

Me too.

Heat speared down Nora's spine, and she was suddenly quite thankful for the lightweight fabric of her favorite summer riding habit, as her body temperature was rising to a feverish degree. "Yes," she whispered, leaning across her saddle toward him. The leather creaked with the movement. "Famished."

Her mare shifted her rump, throwing Nora off balance. She cried out, startled as she lurched toward Rainville. His hands simply tightened on her and settled her back into the seat of her saddle. "There you are," he murmured, slow to let go, trailing his fingers down her arm, lingering.

"Right." Nora cleared her throat and brushed a stray strand of hair from her cheek. Looking at the cloudless sky, she added, "As we were, shall we?"

Cinnamon Sticks nickered and tossed his head slightly, jangling his bridle reins, impatient to carry on. The giant Clydesdale swished his tail and stomped a massive hoof. Her husband shook his head as a low laugh rumbled in his chest. "I think he's perhaps trying to let us know he would like to continue to our chosen destination."

"Oh, I don't know," Nora jested. Her pulse raced at her husband's nearness.

"It's his favorite place to play, and I'm afraid I informed him of the picnic location while tacking him up. He'll be insufferable soon if we don't get him there before his patience wanes."

Delight, pure and unbuffered, poured through her—and Nora laughed at Rainville's sense of humor and his relationship with his mount. "By all means, then, lead the way."

"Cinnamon Sticks would be honored to." He grinned and released his hold on the reins. They dropped to the big stallion's neck. With a slight, nearly imperceptible shift of his powerful legs, Rainville sent his mount in motion. Nora blinked hard, momentarily stunned by the display of his lean, hard thigh muscles flexing.

"Show off," she finally managed, her body tingling with awareness for this man she had never meant to marry.

"Don't blame me," he called over his shoulder as his horse began to trot, amusement ripe in his deep voice. "Blame Cinnamon Sticks."

"I'll do no such thing," Nora countered, nudging her mare into a matching trot. "But I will thank you for the jumping saddle instead of a blasted sidesaddle." Rising in her stirrups, she began to post in rhythm with her horse's gait, taking strain off the mare's back as they covered ground, quickly catching up to Rainville.

"I had a sneaking suspicion that you would rather set a sidesaddle on fire rather than ride with it."

"You're not wrong." Nora laughed—a surprised, short burst. Drawing up alongside her husband, she openly stared at him, taking him in from tawny head to shiny black riding boots. A lifetime of breeding and education had polished Rainville to a particular sheen—one she had mistakenly believed represented the whole of him. It was there in his proud carriage, the fine, aristocratic bones of his face, the distinguished, winged eyebrows he loved to arch so regally. He made such a glossy, golden package of male nobility and privilege that Nora had seen nothing beyond it. Been blinded by it.

Now she saw the playful, quieter man behind the showman duke. And she liked him.

Dear heavens, she liked him.

A lot.

"Race me," Nora blurted out, a surge of emotions propelling her forward in her seat, urging her mare into a canter.

"You're on, minx." The way Rainville said it sent delicious shivers down her spine.

Over the fields they flew, pacing each other, Rainville gaining her complete and utter admiration for his horsemanship abilities when he passed her, and she realized he had not yet picked up his reins. On the contrary, her husband merely held a handful of Cinnamon Stick's long mane in hand, while the reins hung loose about the stallion's neck. The wild, carefree smile on his face sent her heart tripping, stumbling close to a feeling she refused to name.

When they arrived at their destination, Nora was decidedly out of breath. From the ride or the exhilarating feelings tumbling about inside her for this man, she did not know. "That was excellent fun," she declared, bringing her mare to a halt near a large, old tree on the sandy bank of a peacefully winding river. "It has been too long since I've enjoyed a good, hard ride."

Rainville made a strangled, growling sort of sound and dismounted from Cinnamon Sticks, his broad back to her. "I'm happy to oblige you with a hard ride," he replied quietly. "Any time."

The nape of his neck drew her attention as she looked on from her perch on her new mare, loving the way his rich golden hair curled about the collar of his linen shirt. His jacket was neatly tucked away in a pack attached to his saddle. Nora realized she was staring when he turned to her, and she was struck by the intensity in his amber-fire eyes. "What?" she asked, swiping a hand self-consciously over her rapidly flushing cheek.

Rainville was by her side in an instant and his hands were suddenly on her, gripping her waist and lowering her to the ground. He did not let go when her feet touched the earth. "I mean it," he promised, his gaze burning into hers. "*Any. Time.* A good, hard ride is all yours. You have only to ask."

Nora's stomach flipped and her pulse skittered.

She was suddenly well aware that they were not discussing a horse ride, but another kind of ride altogether.

Was she ready?

Chapter Thirteen

They finished eating their packed picnic lunch, and Joss leaned back, bracing his elbows on the picnic blanket spread out over the grass and sand riverbank. Under the shade of a massive old tree, he waited and watched Nora patiently for the subtle signs that she was ready for him. The way a female readied for a male. While not as prolific with women as the gossip rags portrayed him to be, he had his share of experience and knew when a lady wished for his advances or not. And this lady—his *wife*—had warmed to him since their arrival to the river. Her posture had relaxed significantly.

"I want to paint you," Nora burst out, and blushed to her roots when he pointedly raised a brow at her. "I mean, rather, that I want to paint your portrait—with your knowledge." Her hands fluttered, directionless, in front of her. "There are all those new paints and canvases at Somerfield now since the trip to the village yesterday... and I thought... Well..." She blew loosened copper-blonde strands from her gorgeous face and stared over his shoulder to the wide, slow-moving river beyond. "I thought I could perhaps paint a proper portrait of you for... Well, for a wedding gift," she finished on a rush. She waggled slender fingers vaguely at the horses. "She's so very lovely. I'd like to do something in return."

"Nora, you don't have to give me anything." Joss shook his head. "That's not why I did it."

"I know why you did it," Nora replied quietly, and brought her incredible green gaze to his. "Horses are a part of you, a part of who you are. You gave the mare to me in an attempt to share that important part of yourself." She took a deep breath, and his heart squeezed at the knowledge that she understood him. Truly understood him. "I've been thinking about that, and I wish to do the same, and share something of me with you."

There it was: *the sign.*

Everything in Joss tightened and came into acute focus. "I would be honored," he replied with a subtle edge in his tone, and forced himself to remain in his reclining position so as not to startle her. For all her bluster, Nora was far more skittish than he had ever thought possible.

"Well. We must start with a sketch." She brushed her pretty hands together, all brisk business now, and reached for the leather satchel next to her that contained her art supplies. "I'll need you to pose for me. Where should you like to situate yourself?" She glanced up at him and smiled fleetingly. Her mind was clearly a whirl of artistic thought. "You're fine where you are, if you'd rather stay put."

Bringing himself upright, Joss scooted back against the trunk of the enormous shade tree they had eaten under and rested against the bark. Slowly rubbing his back against it, he watched his bride through his lashes, noticed the way she kept sliding him quick, covert glances that had nothing to do with her sketch. Curiosity and nerves flashed behind her eyes, and she inched closer across the blanket toward him.

"I need a closer inspection," she muttered, already in motion with her charcoals across a flat rectangle of parchment. Scooting close enough to touch, Joss purposely remained relaxed and casual while she narrowed her eyes and studied him. "You've the most spectacular eye color," she noted absently as she stroked her hand across the parchment. "I am eager to replicate it with my new oil paints."

"Is that so?" he murmured, and laced his fingers together behind his head, providing some cushion against the rough bark. The rolled sleeves of his linen shirt tugged even higher, leaving his bronzed arms bare to his elbows. Continuing to watch her through his lashes, Joss embraced the ribbon of heat curling in the base of his stomach, enjoyed the flush of arousal.

"Never have I seen another with eye color such as yours. I've itched to paint them for so long now."

"To be fair," he replied, "you have already painted them once."

Nora's head shot up, and her eyes were bright and startled. "Oh, that barely counts." She waved him off and went back to her sketch. "Your eyes were tiny little pools of color. Not at all like what I have in mind now for your portrait."

"Why did you paint me?" The question had been gnawing at him, undermining the trust he felt growing between them. "Of all the men of the *ton*, why me?" Keeping his body relaxed, Joss waited for her response.

For several minutes Nora sketched him in silence, moving her hand at an impressive pace across the parchment. He was uncertain whether she would respond at all when she finally confessed, "I thought you terrible."

Joss quirked a brow and tilted his head. "And now?" His heart thumped a heavy, steady beat while he waited for her answer, realizing how much it mattered to him.

Nora glanced up from her sketch and smiled, slow and devastating. "Now you're not so bad."

"Excellent—high praise indeed," he teased, though coming from Nora, it truly *was* high praise.

"Considering how I felt about you after the fiasco of the Meadowlark Tavern, it really is. I was so furious with you."

Joss noted the use of past tense. "And now?" he asked again, and a part of him recognized the importance of the moment. Though he had not pressed or pushed or even mentioned it, they had yet to fully bind their union. And he was ready.

Christ, he was far past merely ready. He *craved* her.

"Now I'm not," she whispered, and looked at him, her green eyes steady and sure.

"I'm a huge proponent of marriage where the two people do not loathe one another."

"I don't loathe you," she whispered, stilling her drawing hand. "I mean, I did. I decidedly did. But that was before I actually knew you."

"Nora," he said softly, adjusting his long legs as they stretched across the blanket before him.

"Yes?"

Joss lowered his arms and reached out to cup her soft cheek. "I don't think you ever truly loathed me."

"No?" Rounder and rounder her eyes grew. "I didn't?"

With a shake of his head, Joss stroked his thumb across the corner of her plump lips, felt her slight tremble of desire. "No, you didn't." Bringing his other hand to her cheek, Joss cupped her gorgeous face and leaned forward. "You've always wanted me, minx. I think your painting was your way of telling me."

Nora gasped. "It was not!" she protested, her cheeks flushing bright pink.

"Wasn't it?" he pressed.

"No, it wasn't!" his wife cried, raising her hands to wrap them around his wrists. "I was furious with your mistreatment of me!"

"Perhaps," he replied, watching her closely, intently. "But you still wanted me."

"Oh, you're insufferable!" Nora glared at him. "Just like an arrogant man."

"I *am* an arrogant man," he readily agreed. "As a duke, it comes with the title. It doesn't mean I'm incorrect, however."

"*Ohhhh!*" Nora's eyes lit with inner fire. "I'll prove you are wrong."

With that, she gripped his wrists and removed his hands from her cheeks—before throwing herself at him and landing against his solid chest, latching her lips to his. Instantly, sparks erupted inside him, and Joss growled. *Christ, yes.* It was about bloody time.

It seemed a lifetime he had been waiting for this.

Opening instantly, Joss swept his tongue against hers and groaned, loving the taste of her. Decadent and wild. Sweet. Christ, so very sweet. He thrust his hands into her bound hair and fisted, pulling the coppery mass from its pins. "Down," he growled against her lips. "I want it down. Want it in my hands." He wanted it caressing his naked body as she explored him all over.

Possessiveness, primal and fierce, swelled inside him, and Joss took the kiss deeper, the need to claim his wife a driving thunder in his veins. The force of his desire propelled him, had him breaking the kiss and trailing hot kisses over her jaw and down her throat. "I've been so patient, minx. So very patient waiting for you." It had nearly killed him, the wanting and waiting. But he had not uttered a word.

"I meant to prove you wrong," Nora said, tilting her head to provide him better access to the base of her neck. "I'm doing a terrible job of it."

"Mm, that's true, you are." Joss nibbled the delectable, exposed skin above her green riding jacket. "Keep it up."

"Oh, you," his bride sighed. "You complicate things."

"You too, minx." Joss trailed the tip of his tongue up her throat and nipped her stubborn chin. "You're one hell of a complication."

"But you're a theatre owner," she argued, and finally began to explore him with her hands, sweeping them up and over his shoulders until her fingers tangled in his hair. "Drama is kind of your thing."

"I—" he started, but her lips were there and so very alluring, and so he kissed her instead. Their kisses had always been passionate and intense. This time Joss slowed, went languid. This kiss he wanted to savor, this moment. When Nora whimpered and clung to him, he knew she liked it too. And when she wiggled on his lap, shifting until she straddled his hips, Joss knew she was ready for more.

He gave it to her, pressing his straining erection against her core. "You once said that addressing me as Joss would imply an intimacy between us." He found the hem of her riding dress and slipped his hands underneath the layers of fabric, running them lightly up the length of her shapely calves to her thighs. Stopping short of her beautiful womanhood, he slid off to the side and up to grip her lushly rounded hips.

"I did," Nora agreed, and rocked her hips, ground gently against him. Gasping, she added, "I remember that."

"Well," Joss whispered, "I think this is fairly intimate, wouldn't you agree?" The heat from her seared into him, directly through his riding breeches.

"We've still clothes on," Nora countered, shifting restlessly on his lap.

Joss growled and demanded, "Take my tunic off." Leaning forward and giving her room, he groaned when he felt her fingertips brush against his bare stomach. The linen fabric bunched as she lifted it over his head. It came off with a flourish, and she dropped it to the blanket beside them.

"That better?" she asked, running her hands over his bare chest.

"Almost." Joss tipped his chin at her jacket. "Yours too."

She acquiesced and dropped her riding jacket next to his tunic on the blanket. "Now?"

He shook his head, leisurely caressed her hips. "Not yet."

"What then?" she whispered, and licked her lips, her eyes dark and unfocused with passion.

"Pull down your bodice for me," he demanded gently. "I want my mouth on you."

Her sexy little whimper nearly sent him to an early finish. "Like this?" she breathed, tugging her bodice down to expose her beautiful, gloriously full breasts.

"Fuck, yes," Joss growled, gripping her hips. Instantly he had his lips on her, taking her taut pink nipple into his mouth and sucking, then flicking the sensitive tip with his tongue. For several minutes he lavished attention upon them, reveling in their feel and taste, loving the sexy sounds Nora kept making.

When he couldn't handle it anymore, the need to complete their union driving him mad, Joss trailed a hand from her hip to her glorious pussy, finally touching her exactly where and how he wanted to. "Christ, you're exquisite," he whispered. Spreading her, he found her swollen bud and began to rub circles over it with his thumb. Her panting whimpers urged him on, and he circled faster, chasing her sighs. "Say my name," he demanded, needing his name on her lips.

"Joss," she said, devastating him.

Finally.

SUDDENLY NORA WAS on her back, Joss above her with an expression so feral, so untamed, that she gasped. Her duke, completely undone.

Because of *her*.

Goodness, what a sight.

"Joss," she whispered again.

Something dark and seductive flashed in his golden gaze. "Good girl."

Pleasure poured between her thighs. Oh, she *liked* that. Pulling her legs up to cradle him fully, she tugged him back down to her breasts and softly demanded, "More."

He growled, the sound rumbling in his chest as he lowered his head. "What do you say?" Biting her sensitive nipple lightly, he added, "You know what I want."

"Joss," she breathed.

He sucked her nipple into his mouth, flicked his tongue across her peak. "Now say, *Put your mouth on my pussy, Joss.*"

Shock slammed into her, and Nora gasped again, heating with wicked arousal, growing wild at his vulgarity. "You," she panted, wrapping a leg around his waist and pulling his erection closer, "are very naughty."

"And you like it," Joss purred against her bare breasts as his hand moved from her hip to the damp curls between her thighs. "You like it when I talk about your pretty little pussy."

This time Nora moaned.

"Feel how wet you are." A long, strong finger caressed her, ran lightly across her moist opening. He tongued a nipple, moved to the other. "All from a bit of rough language. Tsk-tsk, my lady."

"I—" she started, wriggling against his hand.

"Want my mouth on your pretty pussy." He kissed her hard, deep. "Say it," he urged, "and see what happens."

Nora bit her lip and moaned when his finger found her swollen bud and circled, rubbed her own moisture over her. "I want," she said, rolling her head to the side, but he captured her lips with another scorching kiss, holding her there.

"Tell me," he commanded, low and liquid like fine brandy.

"I want your mouth on my pussy."

"Good, good girl."

Her world lit on fire. Flame after flame licked her body. And then he was there, his beautiful, spoiled mouth on her, licking her as if she tasted sweet as honey. Over and over he stroked his tongue, setting off sparks of sensation that sent her spiraling, soaring higher and higher until she splintered apart. Crying out his name, she clung to him.

"Beautiful," Joss murmured as he rose over her again and positioned himself once again between her legs, his erection full and hot and naked against her flesh. "Now say, *Take me, please.*"

Nora didn't need to be told twice. "Take me, please."

"Fuck yes," he growled, and, in one sure thrust, buried himself deep inside. "I need you, Nora." He anchored himself with a fistful of her hair and shifted, stroked against her. "I need you so fucking much, you don't even know." And then her husband lowered his mouth to hers and took her lips in a kiss so deep she felt it in her very soul.

With each stroke the pressure built again, and Nora let herself go, trusting Joss to keep her close and safe as her world shattered once more into a million sparkling lights. "Joss!" she cried.

"I'm here, love," he promised, his voice raw with emotion. Then he thrust and went rigid, swearing as he found his own release.

Lowering himself to her, Joss rolled his side and pulled her into him, tenderly kissed her neck. "Thank you," he whispered.

"It was… acceptable?" she replied, languid and soft and satiated and suddenly self-conscious. She'd… well, never done *that* before.

His chuckle, so warm and intimate, put her right at ease. "Honey, it nearly killed me."

"Oh, well, that's good," she whispered, snuggling into him.

"You haven't seen anything yet, minx." He kissed her earlobe lightly and added, "Wait until I get you in that big bed in my chambers."

"You won't miss being in it alone?"

"No, Nora," he replied quietly, pulling her impossibly, sweetly close. "I've been waiting for you."

Chapter Fourteen

"I don't believe I have ever seen you quite so rested and happy, Your Grace, as you have been these past days. I daresay it does my heart good."

"Thank you, Winston," Joss said, glancing up from a pile of correspondence on his desk in his study, a smile tugging at his lips. "I have been rather content, I admit."

"The duchess seems rather content, as well." Winston gave him a pointed look, his brown eyes twinkling merrily behind his round spectacles. Crossing over the plush, ornately styled rug in striking shades of blue and yellow, his valet went to the window and openly admired the expansive view of the gardens, the golden stones of the horse barn just visible in the distance. "Somerfield does have that effect on people."

"It does," Joss murmured, only half listening as he opened and read the most recent correspondence. "Although I'd like to think *I* had something to do with the duchess's improved mood."

"Perhaps. It is obvious she has a great deal to do with yours. Your expression in that portrait of you she is painting is quite telling." Winston smiled, clearly pleased. "I am happy for you, Your Grace."

Joss *was* rather joyous, true. Until he read his latest correspondence and frowned. "What the deuce?"

Alerted, Winston hurried to his side. "What is it?"

"It's Castlebury."

"The earl?"

"Yes, the earl." Joss flipped the folded parchment over and continued reading. "It seems that there has been an issue around the theatre in my absence."

"Oh my!" exclaimed the valet. "Not Rhodes!"

"Well," Joss said, "not the theatre itself. It seems that someone has been talking to Goodrich in my absence. Castlebury informs me in this letter that the playwright has been spotted numerous times with the stage manager from Drury Lane over the past two weeks. The earl ran into them personally taking lunch at the Spotted Dog. According to the earl, it appears quite the courtship. He approached Goodrich, but the playwright would tell him nothing other than that he had learned some concerning information. He would not say from whom." Swearing, Joss threw the letter on his desk and pinched the bridge of his nose. "I need to return to London and sort this out." He eyed Winston over his fingers. "If I lose Goodrich, I'm sunk."

"You're financially solvent now," his valet reminded him gently. "Since the wedding."

"Damn it, Winston, it's not about that. The theatre is *my* future, and the future of all the tenants relying on me." He raked a hand through his hair and swore again. "It's for their children and their children's children, don't you see? I'm doing this for the security of the generations to come that depend on the Somerton name and Somerton land, blood relation or hereditary land-dweller, I care not. It's what used to be, what my ancestors had built with the thoroughbreds they bred and raced and sold successfully, until my father destroyed it all through sheer selfishness. My ancestors provided something of substance to the world, not merely a bloody title. They provided something real that mattered." Joss slumped back in his chair. "That's what I'm doing with my theatre. Fixing what my father broke with his neglect and carelessness." He looked at Winston, feeling his resolve rise. "I won't lose Goodrich."

"No, you won't," Winston said, championing him as always, good and loyal friend that he was. "You'll get to London and convince him once and for all to write for Rhodes."

"I don't say often enough how much I value you," Joss stated as he rose from his deep-cushioned leather seat. "But I hope you know how very much I do."

"Oh, well." Winston chortled, his cheeks pinking with pleasure. "Thank you."

"Excuse me, Your Grace," Gomery announced as he knocked on the study door. He opened it and poked his balding head through. "Lord Lambert is here to see you."

Joss groaned. "Blast it, I forgot. I told him to pop round today." Smoothing his gray silk waistcoat, he took a step toward his butler, but his gaze slid to the letter from Castlebury and he stopped. "Winston, please ready me for London and inform the staff. The duchess and I are to leave as soon as possible."

"Should I inform the duchess, Your Grace?" Winston inquired, pushing his spectacles up. "She may wish to say farewell to Lady Claire."

Joss nodded. "See to it."

Gomery cleared his throat. "Should I inform Lord Lambert that you are unavailable, Your Grace?"

"No, I'll speak with him briefly." If the marquess possessed an interest in investing in the theatre, then Joss could not afford to dismiss him without the courtesy of an explanation. For this was the second time Lord Lambert had sought an audience with him.

"Very well, Your Grace." Gomery inclined his head and closed the door behind his retreating form.

"I will notify the duchess and begin the preparations. Mrs. Whipple will wish to inform the upper staff, of course." Winston brushed his hands together and sighed. "I do wish she were less prickly."

Leaving his valet to his personal gripe with the housekeeper, and with urgency quickening his pace, Joss strode from his study and made his way toward the front of the manor, the boot heels of his Wellingtons clicking on the glossy wood floor. A fleeting worry crossed his mind that Nora could still be unsafe in London, but he dismissed it as paranoid. Enough time had passed for the gossip to die down over Anonymous's paintings, and for any angered nobleman to calm and mostly forget.

"Your Grace," Lord Lambert greeted him when Joss stepped into the foyer. "Thank you for meeting with me. I was just admiring this portrait of you. The artist has such a unique style."

Joss glanced at Nora's painting. "Quite, and thank you." He held out a hand and shook Lambert's, noting the strength there with some surprise. "I'm afraid something has come up and I must make haste to London. I apologize for any inconvenience this causes you." Clasping the marquess on the back, he added, "Let me see you out."

A fleeting shadow darkened the nobleman's eyes before he smiled and inclined his head. "Of course, Your Grace. I do hope all is well. Another time, perhaps."

"Thank you," Joss said, ushering the marquess to the door.

He bloody hoped all was well, too.

Chapter Fifteen

Nora had missed London much less than she thought she would. It had seemed an impossibility that she could find contentment and interest in the country, and part of that first carriage ride to Somerfield Park had been spent in worry.

As it turned out, she needn't have worried. Joss's country estate had quickly become her favorite place in all the world. Leaving it had been surprisingly difficult.

Still, she *had* missed her family. Even so, after a week of visits with them and entertainments while Joss handled theatre business, Nora was more than ready to return to the peace and tranquility of Somerfield.

"I'm eager to be on our way," she confessed to Joss as she entered Rhodes Theatre on a sunny afternoon, fresh from a luncheon with her sisters. The noise and activity of Covent Garden and the theatre district felt jarring and discordant to her after the harmony at Somerfield. "I've a portrait to finish painting." She slid her husband a glance and noted his distracted expression. "Joss?"

"Apologies," he muttered as they walked through the halls backstage. "I'm a bit distracted, I'm afraid."

"What has caused you concern?" she asked, her stomach fluttering at his nearness. When his fingers brushed lightly against her bare arm, Nora sucked in air. Her skin tingled. His touch had that effect on her. Would it ever cease? She desperately hoped not.

"Nothing that should concern you, minx." Her husband continued on, his long, strong legs leading her toward the front lobby. He was once again dressed as the showman duke, all peacock-blue velvet jacket and silver waistcoat and entitlement. "I've a playwright that needs more convincing to write exclusively for the theatre, is all."

"Ah, yes. The elusive Thatcher Goodrich, I presume." Lottie could barely stop mentioning the brooding writer ever since her discovery of his connection to Rhodes. "My sister has a list of questions she's compiling on the chance that they should meet. Her thirst for the written word has always astounded me. It's without end."

"Yes, well, if I cannot convince him to commit to Rhodes, then I'm afraid her questions will be far more difficult to answer." Joss grimaced, and Nora could see the tension in his countenance, the slight dark smudges under his golden eyes that hinted at a lack of proper sleep.

"You're quite worried on this matter, aren't you?" It was in the tension of his jaw, the set of his wide shoulders.

"I am," he agreed, and continued to move through the theatre to the extravagantly decorated front lobby. Everywhere Nora looked, she saw opulence. Chandeliers and red velvet and gold satin and glossy marble flooring. What she did not see much of, however—and it surprised her—was art. Very few paintings graced the walls of the plush lobby.

"You'll convince him, I'm certain of it," Nora said, and took a slow spin around, swishing her peach and white skirts about her ankles. "You can be quite persuasive."

"Ah, but am I persuasive enough? That is the real question." Joss cast her a glance, uncertainty in his beautiful gaze.

"You have persuaded me." She smiled. "I was rather unconvinced at the beginning."

"And now?" he asked, slowly walking toward her with his loose-hipped, powerful gait.

"Now I'm a rather big supporter."

And her heart stuttered at the confession.

Her husband reached her, cupped her cheek in a large, strong hand, and kissed her soundly. "Thank you," he murmured, his eyes hinting at an emotion she dared to hope was love.

Perhaps Joss could love her after all.

Perhaps her painting had brought her something good—not ruination and regret, as she had feared. Truly, when he gazed at her like that, like she *mattered*, she believed it was possible. *Wanted* it to be.

"I've been thinking," Nora said, and gestured to the lobby surrounding them, "that you could do with some art on the walls in here."

"Is that so?" Joss asked quietly, glancing around them. "I assume you know an artist?"

"It so happens that I do. I would be happy to paint something."

"I think you've painted enough, minx." The way he said it had her back stiffening.

Nora narrowed her eyes on her husband and stepped from his embrace. Her stomach sank. "What is that supposed to mean?"

"It means that you've painted enough, that you've had your fun." Joss raked a hand through his thick mane of hair. "After all the noblemen you've mocked, I cannot see putting your artwork in the theatre. What if one of them recognizes your work?"

A hot ball of disappointment congealed in the pit of her stomach. "I did not realize you viewed my artwork as mockery."

Joss threw up his hands and burst out, "How else am I supposed to view it, Nora? For Christ's sake, you've spent the past months doing nothing but create paintings to humiliate others." He thumped his chest with a fist. "Me included."

"I never—" she started, but he cut her off.

"Save it. I am not a simpleton, easily misled." The scowl upon his beautiful face nearly scorched her with its intensity. "You cannot expect me to leap at the opportunity, Nora. I'm in a precarious enough position with the theatre as it is, and I still lack the security of Goodrich. Showcasing your paintings here would be far more detrimental than beneficial."

"I did not mean for you to hang *those* paintings, but new ones," Nora whispered, her heart starting to ache in a way she'd never felt before. It *hurt*. "Is that... is that what you truly think of me?"

"Not you, Nora." Joss shook his head. "Your art."

"Oh!" Nora cried out. Tears stung her eyes as emotion welled inside her. "You are cruel."

"*I'm* cruel?" he asked, incredulous. "What about you? You're the one who decided that it was fine to humiliate another human being for sport!"

"Not for sport!" she shouted back, pain slicing through her. "It was never for that reason."

"Right." He sniffed, all haughty. And it was clear by the hard glint in his eyes that he did not believe her. "Because I was such a monster."

"I never said that!"

"Oh, but you did. When you painted that... that *painting*, you had already determined I was the worst sort of man."

"I didn't realize you were that upset about it." Nora crossed her arms tightly across the front of her as tears spilled down her cheeks.

"Why in bloody hell wouldn't I be upset? It nearly ruined me, Nora!"

"But it didn't," she whispered, feeling small and guilty and ashamed. "It didn't ruin you at all."

"Only because I was forced to marry you instead!"

Nora gasped and her heart split in two. "I'm so sorry that I was such a horrible punishment!" Spinning on the heels of her walking boots, Nora searched for the main entrance to the theatre and rushed toward it.

"Nora, wait!" Joss called after her, but she was deaf to his plea.

Bursting out into the bright sunshine, Nora squinted against the glare. Wiping furiously at the tears running down her cheeks, she turned left outside the theatre, hurrying toward her waiting carriage. "Oh, that man! He's... Oh, he is the worst!" Damn him for breaking her heart.

"Nora!"

Ignoring her husband's call, she started to run toward the carriage, sobbing openly now. Two more carriages to pass and then hers—and she could leave. Why, she could leave London if she wished! Somerfield Park seemed the perfect destination. Only a few more steps...

A hand came out of nowhere, latching on to Nora's arm, the grip tough as iron, and yanked her right off her feet. "There you are, little bitch."

"Nora!" Joss bellowed behind her. *"Nora!"*

She screamed and was silenced with a cold, brutal hand across her mouth. Glancing up as she felt herself shoved into a carriage, she caught a glimpse of her kidnapper. "You bastard!" she cried, and rocked back from the force of the slap across her cheek.

"Stop him!" she heard her husband yell as the carriage lurched into motion. "Stop that carriage!" And then he roared, *"Lambert has my wife!"*

"So we finally meet, *Anonymous*."

Lambert's hand connected with her cheek once more and Nora's world faded to black.

Chapter Sixteen

Lambert's carriage sped down Tavistock Street away from Joss, taking Nora with it. Fear and fury erupted in equal measures inside, and he wasted little time. Spotting Cinnamon Sticks harnessed to one of his carriages, Joss ran to the Clydesdale and barked orders at his driver, James. "Unhitch him now! *Now!*" *Good God, Nora.* His Nora. Why would he take her?

The painting.

"Faster!" Joss shouted, grabbing harness bits and yanking to speed the process. "They're getting away! Fuck. *Fuck!*"

The marquess was a dead man. If he touched a single hair on Nora's head…

"Done!" James hollered from the far side of Cinnamon Sticks. "This side is done!"

The big bay stallion stomped, twitched his ears, and snorted, sensing the urgency as he was freed of the harness. Joss grabbed a fistful of mane, saying to his trusted steed, "I need your help, friend," and kicked out a leg, swinging up onto his horse's back from the wrong mounting side, knowing the stallion wouldn't shy away. "Go," he ordered his mount before he had even settled into position. Cinnamon Sticks leapt into the road and powered after Lambert's carriage.

"A bridle, Your Grace!" called his driver behind him. "You need a bridle!"

"No time!" Joss hollered, leaning low over his horse's neck, a fistful of mane in hand, and squeezed tight with his knees. "I trust you, Cinnamon Sticks. Go now. *Go!*"

His mount raced forward at full speed, a mighty gallop that propelled them down Tavistock after the rapidly disappearing carriage. Hooves pounded the ground as he weaved around slowly moving carriages, deaf to the angry and offended shouts aimed in his direction.

"Watch it, you blasted dandy!" said a costermonger when Cinnamon Sticks avoided a parking carriage by taking the sidewalk and brushing against his cart. Several pedestrians shouted and leapt to the side.

Joss ignored them all, fear for his Nora almost choking him. "Faster, Cinnamon Sticks. Faster!"

"What are you, crazy?" bellowed a man in a black beaver hat after plastering himself to the nearest building out of harm's reach. He shook an angry fist in the air.

Up ahead, Lambert's carriage whipped left, rocking hard enough to raise it onto one wheel. "No!" It couldn't roll, it couldn't. Not with his wife inside.

I never told her I love her.

"Damn it," Joss swore as pain exploded in his chest. "Damn it! She should know."

Please. Please. I need her.

Urging Cinnamon Sticks on, Joss gripped tight as the extraordinary horse obeyed his every command—without saddle or bridle. "That's my boy!" he said after his mount leapt straight over a man bent down retrieving a parasol for his companion and kept going, not once breaking stride. Utterly unflappable. Joss's hero.

The stallion pounded after the runaway carriage, street after street. Down Strand they raced. Without the weight of a carriage holding him down, Cinnamon Sticks steadily gained ground, and soon they were within a few carriage lengths of Lambert—close enough for Joss to see Nora's copper-blonde head snap back when a slap from Lambert rocked her into the cushioned seat.

Rage flooded Joss. "Bastard!" Lambert would die for laying a hand on his wife.

With his horse breathing heavy with exertion, Joss pushed on, desperate to save Nora. As they raced along, it soon became obvious that the marquess was headed for Hyde Park. Joss was forced to detour around a slow-moving hack. Cursing the lazy driver, he pressed with his legs, signaling to his horse which way to go. Around the left they maneuvered, just as the entrance to Rotten Row in Hyde Park appeared. Joss noted all those pleasure riders and the narrow opening between thick wooden posts with trepidation. Lambert's carriage was going too fast to safely make the entrance.

"*Nora!*" His throat ached from the force of his scream.

For a blink—a mere moment—Joss lost sight of Lambert's carriage as Cinnamon Sticks pushed hard and strong around the sluggish hack. Its folding roof was fully extended and blocked him from seeing the team of horses pulling Lambert and Nora turn toward Rotten Row— then the wheels of the coach hit a rut and sent it into the air.

"No!" Joss yelled, watching on in horror as the carriage tilted in midair. A wheel splintered and sent wooden bits shooting dangerously through the air. His heart stopped as the conveyance came down on its side with a deafening crash and flipped over twice before rolling to a stop in a cloud of dust. "Nora!" *Oh God,* his love.

Cutting across the road, mindless to anything but the knowledge that his wife was inside, Joss leapt off Cinnamon Sticks when he neared the wreckage and hit the earth at a flat run. "*Nora!*" Dust billowed around him as he closed the last bit of distance.

He was reaching for the broken carriage door when it swung open and Lambert climbed out, bloody and bleeding and wielding a sword. "Back off," the marquess bit out, spitting out saliva and blood and several teeth. Stumbling toward Joss, Lambert swung the blade wildly, his dark eyes glassy with pain and insanity. "Back the bloody hell off!"

"I just want my wife." Joss raised his hands, palms out, to show that he was unarmed. "Let me go to her."

"Never!" the marquess cried, and swished the thin fencing sword at him. Blood seeped freely from a wound in his side, and the whole front of his shirt was soaked deep red. "You don't understand what she's done!"

"I know about the painting," Joss said, trying to locate a way around Lambert to get to his wife. "Nora!" he called out. "Nora, can you hear me?"

He heard it then, the slightest sound. A whimper, really. Nothing more. But it belonged to his wife. And that gave Joss precious hope.

"Hold on, love, I'm coming for you!"

"No, you're not," sneered Lambert, his face contorted in pain, the wound in his side draining the very life from him. "That bitch tried to humiliate me, tried to ruin me with her painting. You don't ruin a Revivalist!" The marquess stumbled toward him, waving his foil wildly about. "A Revivalist ruins you!"

Lambert was a Revivalist. A goddamn murdering Revivalist. And he had planned to kill Nora for her painting.

Joss saw fury. Blind fury that he released on a roar so raw and visceral that it stopped Lambert. *"You won't touch my woman!"*

"I already did." Lambert smiled darkly, and then the edges turned down into a grimace and he stumbled, coughed blood that dribbled down his chin. But when Joss made a move toward the carriage and Nora, Lambert whipped the foil toward him with shocking speed, halting him instantly. "She deserved it and so much more. Lady Lingbottom told me what truly transpired between you two in the garden that night at Claremoore's ball. Oh yes, she saw you. Saw that Castlebury's dearest daughter had a painting of *you* too. Yet instead of enduring humiliation together with me as brethren wronged, facing the *ton,* you went and married the enemy. Became my enemy too. And you tossed Seraphina over for the brazen bitch. Though I do thank you for that. She pleasures better than any lightskirt." He twitched his blade, lightning fast, when Joss glanced once more over his shoulder toward the wrecked carriage. "Don't do it, Rainville. I'll gut you like a fish if you make one more move toward that stupid whore."

Of course Seraphina was involved in this. Joss *had* seen her in Somerton that day outside the art store. The two of them must have been plotting. He pushed that revelation away, to be dealt with after Nora was safe.

"Lambert," he tried, tone strained.

The blade swished before his nose. "Like a bloody fish, Duke. One false move from you…"

Joss believed him, knew the marquess was more than capable. His encounter with the Revivalists weeks ago had demonstrated that. Lambert would slice him in two and not even blink.

"Joss?" He heard Nora's weak, terrified voice, and it filled him with purpose. Strength. *Love.*

"I'm coming, love! Just hold on!" he called to her, needing her, loving her so much he could scarcely contain it.

"You'll die first," Lambert spat, advancing on him with murder in his eyes. His foil glistened sharp in the sunlight.

And that was when Joss's horse saved his life. From the corner of his eye, he caught a blur of motion, a whirl of brown and white as Cinnamon Sticks reared with a piercing neigh and struck with his mighty hooves, sending Lambert flying backward through the air. On a scream, the marquess landed, impaling himself on his own sword. He gasped two times and then went still, gasping no more.

Joss didn't wait to see if he was truly dead and scrambled into the carriage to retrieve his wife. His one and only love. He found her hunkered in a tiny ball and brought her from the wreckage, cradling her gently on the grass just past the edge of Rotten Row. "Nora, love, you're safe."

"I—I'm so sorry," she whispered. Her beautiful eyes fluttered open and filled with tears. "I'm so sorry for my paintings."

"Bugger your paintings." Joss held her in his arms, knowing he would never, ever let her go. "You're alive, and that's all I care about. *You.* My wife. My love."

"Your... love?" The expression of sweet hope on her face undid him.

"I love you, Ceranora Rainville," he blurted. "I love you so bloody much. And I was so scared when I saw Lambert take you. Paint whatever you want, whenever you want. I never should have been such an arse about it, and I'm sorry. Can you forgive me?"

"I already have." Her small, tender smile humbled him. Honored him.

A gentle nickering sound, and they turned as Cinnamon Sticks appeared next to them and lowered his massive head to them, sniffing and nudging them with his soft muzzle. "Thank you, my friend." Joss leaned his head into his horse's, grateful to this magnificent creature for the rest of his days. "You saved her. Just like I knew you would."

"My heroes." Nora placed one hand on Joss's cheek and one on Cinnamon Stick's furry jaw. "My absolute heroes. I love you both so much."

Cinnamon Sticks nickered his approval and nibbled lightly at her hair. She laughed gently and flinched, wincing in pain.

"You're hurt." If Lambert wasn't already dead, Joss would kill him.

"I'm fine. Bruises, is all. I'll mend."

"I love you, Nora."

"I love you, Joslin Bonaventure." His bride grinned, her beautiful eyes sparkling, and he knew then and there he would spend the rest of his life making her smile like that. "Can I call you Bonny?"

Joss smiled and leaned down to kiss the woman he loved more than life. The woman he deeply and truly adored. "Only if I can call you Norabell."

"Agreed," she whispered, pulling his lips to hers.

Nora could call him anything she wanted to. Anything at all. So long as she called him hers.

Epilogue

Three months later
Rhodes Theatre
London

"You made quite the muddle of things, didn't you, my girl?" the Earl of Castlebury said with a shake of his white head, rubbing a fist against his chest as he smiled, appearing quite pleased. "But it turned out all right in the end." Pointing around the lobby of the opulent theatre at the throng of patrons, he added, "Seems my investment is paying off nicely."

"Don't be crass, Winslow." Nora's mother laughed. "No one wishes to talk business while enjoying an evening of entertainment." She sipped her glass of champagne and leaned toward Nora. "Especially not when we've two talented daughters being showcased."

"Did Carenza decide to reveal herself, then?" Lottie whispered, glancing about to ensure no one overheard. She looked lovely and so grownup in her ice-blue frock with her long, wheat-tone hair pinned into a complicated updo. "Also, has anyone seen Thatcher Goodrich? I've a list of questions to ask him, and I'm eager to start."

Nora caught sight of her husband across the crowded lobby, tall and dashing in his red velvet jacket and glossy boots, and her stomach flipped excitedly. Would it always be this way with Joss? Giddy and so full of happiness and love that she could barely keep it all contained? Sometimes she feared she might just float away. "He is the gentleman standing between Joss and Damon over there by the entrance to the upper balconies."

"Are you jesting with me?" Lottie's mouth dropped open. "That one there, with the dark hair pulled back at the nape of his neck and brooding countenance?"

"That's the one." Nora laughed. "Why, does his appearance concern you?"

"No, no," Lottie protested, eyes locked on the famous playwright. "His appearance is quite fine."

"Oh look, your brothers have finally arrived," Lady Castlebury exclaimed happily. "It is good of them to make time for pleasurable activities."

"My goodness, he's coming this way," Lottie whispered, her eyes growing bigger with every step the playwright made toward them. "I… I must get some air."

Nora intended to stay her sister with a hand, but her husband appeared at her side and all rational thought left her head. "Hello." She smiled dreamily up at her duke. Her husband. Her *love*.

"I've come bearing excellent news," Joss said into her ear, sending a delicious shiver down her spine. "Your paintings are a smashing success. So much so that the Earl of Dunbart just now inquired about the purchase of your landscape of the hills of Somerfield Park. Before that, Lady Billows asked about commissioning the artist for a personal project. And before *that*, Sir Marley made a very generous offer on your painting of Cinnamon Sticks and offered an excellent price for you to paint his own mount. In fact, he wishes all of his horses to have their own portraits."

"You jest!" Nora gasped.

He kissed her neck just below her ear and murmured, "It's true. All of it. You're about to become a very wealthy and busy artist, minx."

"I—" Nora fanned herself, suddenly short of breath. "I—"

"It's an incredible feeling, isn't it?" Joss nuzzled her neck, clearly caring not at all who noticed—and neither did she.

Life was for living in bold, vivid color. Out loud, for all to see.

"I'm so proud of you," her husband whispered, and she felt it, knew his feelings were true.

"Thank you for supporting me and my work. I love you," she whispered with a smile in her voice, and patted his cheek. "You're a good man, Bonny."

"Nora," her husband growled in warning. "We've talked about this."

"All right, *fine*." She glanced up at Joss, her love for him shimmering bright inside. "But you owe me another portrait session after I finish capturing the light in the stairwell at Barlow House with my oils. And this time I'm thinking nude."

"Subject or the painter?"

"Both, of course." Nora laughed, so very full and happy with life's unexpected blessings. One scandalous painting and kiss later, here she was.

And it was *exactly* right.

The End

About the Author

Jennifer Seasons started her career writing contemporary romances for Avon and is the author of several popular contemporary and Regency historical romances. Born in California, Jennifer has lived all over the West and now resides in the mountains of Massachusetts with her husband and their children. A dog and several cats keep them company. A lover of autumn, cozy cardigans, and coffee, Jennifer can often be found writing her novels by hand in notebooks, bundled in said cardigan with a steaming mug of dark roast nearby. When she's not writing, Jennifer enjoys running, hiking with her family, gardening, and lounging in a comfy spot with a good book and a homemade chocolate chip cookie or two.

Amazon – https://www.amazon.com/stores/Jennifer-Seasons/author/B00D8GZ5EE
Twitter – https://twitter.com/JenniferSeasons

Printed in Great Britain
by Amazon